# PIPER

## QUEEN'S BIRDS OF PREY BOOK 4

# KATHI S. BARTON

This is a work of fiction. Names, characters, places, and incidents are products of the author's imagination or are used fictitiously and are not to be construed as real. Any resemblance to actual events, locations, organizations, or persons, living or dead, is entirely coincidental.

**World Castle Publishing, LLC**
Pensacola, Florida
Copyright © Kathi S. Barton 2020
Paperback ISBN: 9781953271365
eBook ISBN: 9781953271372
First Edition World Castle Publishing, LLC, November 9, 2020
http://www.worldcastlepublishing.com
Cover: Karen Fuller
Editor: Maxine Bringenberg

# Prologue

The castle was going down, thanks wholly to her birds. Queen Dante sat upon her horse and watched as stone after stone crumbled to the ground. In a matter of moments, not only were the walls to the fort destroyed, but the king inside his castle was dead. Turning her mount, she headed back to the encampment to ready herself for the long ride home. The birds joined her not half an hour later, their large bodies covered in dust and blood.

"You have done well, my darlings." They could understand her and she them, but no one else could. She had made them what they were, and she would be the only one to control them. "Have you fed well on his dying cattle? How does it serve a man to have his food dying? His people, they were fed no better, I saw."

The falcon—she had never named them—told her

the people were headed west. In a few months, probably less, they would all be dead too. It bothered them when the people suffered because of the king or queen of the castle, but it was to be. Dante could not care for any more people in her own keep.

No one would attack her keep. If they tried, she knew them to be stupid or drunk on their own mead. She had her birds, all of them bigger than life, made large by the magic that she gave them. Looking at them as they landed around her, forever keeping her safe, she wondered why she had not thought of it sooner when her king was still alive.

"I would have set you upon him. You could have eaten him for your dinner. Though I suspect it would have given you a great deal of belly pains." The hawk told her she was lucky he had died the way he had. No one would come for her if she had killed him. "Yes, that is very true. But I suffered greatly when he was living. No children either to give me comfort in my olden age. Though they might have been just like him, and that would have been too much to bear."

She would never marry again. Love wasn't anything she searched for. Not that she didn't have someone to warm her bed on occasion. But it was nice to be able to send them on their way when she had finished with them. Her heart belonged to no one, and she would not have another man take her to bed by force. All would be well—no one would threaten to come and take over her home. That was a certainty.

The hawk used her beak to put delicate things upon the backs of the others. There was aplenty this time. Barrels and smoked meats. Pottery that they would use like it wasn't worth a king's gold. They raided the castle each time they conquered. Hawk was the best at getting in and out before they took the place to the grounds.

The eagle took off toward home. She would let the people know Dante was returning simply by showing up. They would have a feast this night. The food upon her back would feed them for many days. The barrels of spices, hoarded in the lower levels of the castle, would go a long way toward helping them trade for what they did not grow.

The phoenix, by far the most deadly of her birds, shed her feathers in anticipation of getting new ones. After a battle, she would become anew, each time getting stronger, her feathers, brilliant now, would be brighter still. She could flame a fire so hot that stone would crumble under a man's feet. The ground would no longer hold a seed within its belly to produce food, and she could kill a man with a single breath so there would be nothing left of his body.

She loaded the last of her things onto the back of the owl. She might be small, Dante had always thought, but she could carry more than her own weight. And she would pick up her horse, used to flying through the sky like a bird himself, and take him back to the castle. He would be fed and groomed before she ever landed on the ground.

The vulture squawked at her, and she turned to look at the two men there. They looked as if they might have been about to kill her, but the sight of such large birds threw them off their duty. In no time at all, the vulture snapped both of them up and swallowed them down. A gruesome sight, but one that filled her heart with joy. She was safe again. The vulture took off once she was loaded up.

"Well, my falcon, it is just you and I left." She told her she was still armed. "Yes, well, probably not too bad of an idea seeing that they nearly shot us."

The falcon laid her body to the ground. She was the only one fitted with a seat, one that Dante rode on. Scouring the area, Dante always made sure the places she camped were as neat and clean as she'd found them — sometimes in better shape.

As she climbed on the back of her bird, she held her breath. "I do hate the height. I should have thought this through when I turned you into my warriors." Her laughter, should there have been someone around to hear it, might have given the impression that she was insane. "Homeward, my love, and we shall eat well tonight."

She took no one with her on her fights, except the birds. That was why, she believed, her people were so loyal to her. She protected them, fed them better than herself, and made sure there was plenty for them to trade for things she did not provide for them.

The soil was rich and would give forth a bounty like no other gardens. Flowers woven into pretty things were traded as well. There was a smithy as well as a doctor, who doubled as a dentist. They had even acquired a gravedigger, who also doubled as a man who made markers.

A single merchant came by on occasion. His wagon, filled when he arrived, would be near empty when he left. He brought the latest news with him and any posts he had been asked to bring. He would also, for a small coin, take out posts for the next time he was in the keep of a relative or friend.

And today, there was such a missive. But it was for her, from someone she had hoped never to hear from again — the king of the land, the only man she answered to, though it wasn't with any kind of happiness on her part.

After the others were settled down, the food that had been brought put into storage, she sat down and wasn't surprised that the falcon came to see her. The room she was in — the throne room, for lack of a better term — had no roof and six perches for the birds when they wished to see her. Otherwise, they sat upon the top of the castle turrets, watching for anything that might befall them.

"I am to wed. The king of the land, he has decided my castle is the best there is, and he will marry me himself." The falcon asked about his castle. "He says it will be his son's, which he has none of as yet. His last five wives only gave him daughters, from what I have heard, and they did not last long afterwards."

The falcon asked her what she would do. Dante knew what would happen to her should he come here. He would kill her. Being in her fortieth summer, she was much too old to bear any children now, and he would be better with a younger bride. One that could birth him the sons he wanted.

"He will kill me; we both know that. And you six will kill him or be killed. I worry so much for the people here too." She thought of several plans and threw them out. It was in her head that if she were to die, then she would do so on her own terms. "I will need a day to think on this. In the meantime, he says he will be here in the new year. That will give us a month to provide for the people and make sure they are not harmed."

~*~

Dante worked as hard as the rest of her people. With her hair up in a rag, she didn't look any different than any of the men and women that toiled with her. There was much to be done in the little time they'd been allotted. Today they were drying all the beef and goat meat they had. It would last them for several months, and where she was sending them for safety, they'd need that extra time. Long enough for them to breed more of their cattle and goats so there would always be food for them to eat.

"What of the dried herbs that are left, my lady? There

are barrels of it packed away for the trip and already on its way to the new home. Shall we put what is left in a bag to go tonight?" She shook her head. "There are no more barrels until the morn. The copper is working as fast as he can, making more. What shall we do?"

"Leave them. There is very little, correct?" The man said that there wasn't enough for a good strong stew. "Good. They will think you all died off from lack of planning, and that will keep you safe for a longer time. Leave it for them, so when the keep and castle are in ruin, the king will understand why."

Not that anyone was going to be coming to the castle to live, she thought. Things were in motion that would make sure that everything here was gone well before the lands were walked upon again.

Dante looked to the sky when a dark shadow fell over her. Her hawk was making her way to the village Dante had set up. Long ago, Dante had purchased the lands far from where she was now and put them in the name of Mercy Dante. She knew so much about all their futures that it made her so sad to know she'd not be there to see it happen.

"My lady?" She looked at her man of arms, a man that had very little work to do but was brave and true to her. "We have plenty of things to go on the next load if you have a desire to send it on. Do you still wish for some of the armed men to go with them this time? I'm to understand we're to fell trees for homes."

"Yes, that would be good. How many men can you spare today?" He told her all that she had. "Then send them on. I know some of you are frightened to ride the birds, but you should have no fear. They would no more harm you than they would me." He nodded and looked at her hawk. "I shall send you all on her. She is the gentlest of the six of them."

The carrier had been fashioned a week ago. It had upset her that it had taken so long to get right, but it was safe now, and that was all she wanted. There were only a few short weeks left to get the people gone from here with all that would keep them safe. Now all she had to do was make sure the birds didn't know the last of her plans.

The platform had been made from several drawbridges from castles they'd taken over. She had known that saving them would be helpful, but it had taken a great deal more work than she'd thought to put them together and have her fishermen weave a netting to carry it with. After several tries and failures, the carrier worked.

Loading up the men on the first run of people, she noticed they had put the several men that were afraid of the ride in the middle. One of them, a hardy man otherwise, had been knocked out with much wine. It had been funny to all around that it took so little of the wine to do that to him. But they didn't know she'd given him a bit of magic to help him travel. All was well when her hawk took off with the several dozen men to start on the homes that would be needed.

Barrels would be next. They had been sealed by magic that would keep them well preserved. The other birds, her warriors for all time, had been taking jewels and other items to a cave she had also covered in magic. It would help the people of the new village for as long as they lived, well beyond her body being nothing but dust.

Dante watched as several more people were taken to the new village. She would allow them to name their new place so long as it would never be attached to the name of the castle. That would be bad for them and would bring much trouble onto their heads.

When her hawk landed, she went to ask how things were progressing.

"Well, my lady. They were no more off the platform for seconds when they started to work. I believe you were good to get them started on this. 'Tis only early winter, so they should be able to have a few of the buildings up before the rest are moved." Dante agreed with her. No one else could understand the birds but her and the other birds. It had, she knew, kept everyone safe all these years. "I can only make two trips there and back, my lady. 'Tis not a long way by the way we fly, but the pack is heavy. Please forgive me for that."

"You have nothing to be sorry for, my bird of prey. You have done one more than I had hoped for this day. And when the others have finished their tasks for me in carrying away the riches and other things they will need, it will take no time at all to move the rest. Nay, you have done well this day in taking the men, and then the food to feed them while there." Her hawk, who would someday be called Blaze, bowed before her.

Stacking up the loads that would be going on the platforms, she could see that they'd be taking away the last of it only the day before the king was to arrive. Dante was glad now that she'd had such good people working for her. They asked nothing as to why they were doing this but just did it. When in reality, it was all for them and her birds.

Dante knew the king would never make it here. His ship and all his bounty would be deep in the waters he crossed to kill her and take her castle. The man was a fool to think she would easily do what he wanted. It would not be her that killed him—it would be her bird. But in the event that it didn't go the way she'd seen it, the plan to move her people was the best way to keep them safe.

Wiping at a tear, she looked around the keep she'd worked so hard to keep everyone safe in. It was then she saw her son.

Duncan was everything she was and more. Each time she saw her son, she would give him a little more of herself, teach him something of running a castle. He knew what he was to her and that Mary was doing her a great favor in keeping him safe. Duncan would be a greater king than she ever was a queen, just the way it should be. She was glad now that she'd told him he was to be mated to one of her birds.

Leaving him to his work, she entered the castle to see what else was there that she could easily live without. There was very little left as it was, but she moved from room to room to make sure nothing of any value was left behind.

The only thing she could see in the great room was the painting of herself. Dante wished so many times that she could have put her son there with her, but it was not to be. It would have been foolhardy to think she'd be able to keep him safe if she was to put out there that he'd been born. Other kingdoms would have done a great many things to capture him to bring her to heel. Dante would do anything to keep him safe, including submitting to a man again. A thing that she would never do again in her lifetime.

"I shall give this to our falcon." She turned her head enough to find Duncan behind her, and the doors closed to anyone walking around. "She will be a great person, I think. Sour to many except the one she will love."

"You have seen this?" Duncan said he'd seen a great many things. "Well, you know as well as I that it might not turn out the way we see it. There can be changes, you know."

"This I am aware of. As well as you not living past the last person being taken from here." She turned to look at him then, trying to see just what he was seeing. "I shall forever miss you, Mother."

It was the first time he'd called her that. Her heart was so tender of late that she would burst into tears at all that would be gone in so short of time. Hugging him to her, she felt the strength in his body, which was getting stronger daily. He knew how to work and did it without complaint.

"I have been writing a book. It is just for you, my son. You will know things I have known for some time. It will replenish the riches I have put aside for you. Also, tell you how to keep the birds safe should they need it." He nodded. "I will give it to Mary on the day you travel. I do not want the others to know you are my son, even after all is finished here."

"They will only know me as a man you trusted. But I will need to tell them at some point. This you know as well as I. I will be their king when they need me." She nodded, tears flowing quickly now. "Mother, you do know I will take care that they are as safe as you made them here, don't you?"

"I do, my son. I know that better than you could. You are not anything like your father, a cruel and terrible man. When you marry, and you will, I want you to know she will only love you if you give her your heart. It's important you do that for her." He said he would. "Let her strength help you when you know you are not armed to do it on your own. She will love you more and respect you forever for that."

"Will she be stronger than me, Mother?" Dante told him she was sure of it. "Then I will be for her what you have been for these people. A person of worth. I promise you I will also protect her forever."

"That is all anyone can do for their mate, my child." He hugged her, something that neither of them were able to do often. "I shall miss you, Duncan. Much more than I could ever explain to you. Go forth, protect all the people of your kingdom, and do what I say. Love your mate more than anyone, including yourself, and the two of you will be able to move mountains."

~*~

New Town, what they had begun to call the new place they were living, looked like any other town in the country. The only difference was, this one was only several weeks old. To Dante, it looked as if it had been established long ago. She was pleased with the work her people had given the place she'd moved them to.

"My lady? There is a problem in one of the homes we've put up. I know how to fix it, but the man living in it, he said he will be fine with it. To have his own home was more than he could have hoped for." The queen of the people asked Barron what was the issue. "He has five daughters, my lady, and we've somehow put him in a house with only one bedroom. There are ones he could use, but he insists it be used for the other families."

"I shall speak to him. Is it Donald, the mule man?" Barron nodded, his face nearly touching the ground;

he was bent so low. "Stand up, man. I believe I have pointed out this is not a time for formality. We must all work together for the greater good of the people. I shall speak to him now. Then I must, as you know, return to the castle for the final loading."

Along the way to speak to Donald, she was stopped no less than twenty times to be thanked for the things she'd provided for the people here. Without making the great move, Dante knew all of them would be killed. Because of their loyalty to her as queen of the castle, the king of these realms, a tyrant of a man, would have ordered them all butchered as soon as he killed her on their wedding night. Not that she was assured of him coming here. This was her plan, a way to keep them safe if she had read her dreams incorrectly.

"My lady? I have yet to put on a pot for tea, but you must join us in it." Dante was not one to hold back when she had something to say. She told Donald she wanted him to take a larger home. "Oh, my lady. Barron should never have bothered you with this. We are quite happy with where we are."

"But you have six people in a single man's home, Donald. What, I ask you, will the man who was supposed to be in this house do with a home with many bedrooms? He will be overwhelmed, trying to keep them clean while you are smashed up in this one bedroom chamber with your little girls." Donald looked at his daughters, beautiful little ones that were his pride and joy. "There is a home just over the road that you shall be moved to. I insist. Your daughters will share two bedrooms, and you will have your own. I know for a fact, sir, that your snore is legendary. For your daughters to have a good sleep, you will need to be far from them. Do you not agree?"

"Yes, my lady." He moved just a little closer, and in a low voice, spoke to her. "I did not wish to cause you any undue trouble. You have given all of us a chance to survive this, and I wanted to be sure you knew I was ever so grateful for it. I'm as happy here with you and yours as I ever was in the castle keep, my lady. Incredibly happy."

"I'm glad you're happy here, Donald. You are a good man and a man that cares well for his daughters. I shall have the men move you to the new home. It will give me a good feeling knowing you have plenty of room for yourself and your family." He thanked her. "Your daughters, sir, they will be safe here. You need anything, you make sure you contact Barron."

"Thank you, my lady. If there is ever anything I can do for you, you need only to ask. I am and will be indebted to you for the rest of my days." Dante felt her eyes water up with the man's word. Her life, she knew, was only a short time away from ending. "Thank you very much."

The little girls curtsied at her, and she had to move on. It broke her heart every time she saw small children. She so wanted to hold her own. Telling Donald she'd have the men move him once again, she moved toward the long house that would serve as a church for the people and a meeting place for them to gather should they need to.

Her eagle was awaiting her when she returned to the now all but abandoned castle.

"You have done well, my heart. You of all the birds I have are the one I worry most about." The eagle asked her why. "You are so much like me. Hard when you're needed to be, too soft when it comes to our people. I fear someday it will harm you in ways that not even I could fix."

Her eagle, like the other birds, had been a huge part of getting the people moved. If not for them, there would be no way she could have done this. It would have meant certain death for all of them, including her own son.

Going to the throne room, she sat upon the floor. Dante had moved her chair to the caves for the others to sell off should no one want it. But because she could see into the future, just bits and pieces, she knew at least one of them would want such a monstrosity.

"When this is finished, soon now, I will give you and the others magic to keep you safe from others who would try and capture you." Her eagle asked what sort of magic. "You will be able to blend into situations you wouldn't normally consider a problem. There will be those situations, too. For the things I have seen, you all will have trouble from those around you."

She laid back on the cold stone. The castle had been forged so long ago, Dante could not remember who had been the person who erected it. Now, as she looked up into the night sky, the roof here long since removed, she thought of what was going to happen in the coming days.

"He has set sail and is nearly here. The king of all the lands is coming to claim not just my castle and my wealth, but my birds as well. There are many people on the vessel that carts his bottom here who have no desire to be his servants. If only I could have saved them as well." The eagle, standing upon her perch built just for her, reminded Dante she could not save them all. "In this, I wish it was wrong to have thought that. They will suffer these people. They are suffering, for there is nothing to do to appease the king to find favor with him. There are so few that he has not made suffer by lashing them on their backsides. Too many of them have died in his foolishness to make me his wife for such a short time."

Listening to her eagle squawk at her about the king and idiocy, Dante thought of her impending death. It would be a sad affair to her son and the birds he would one day claim as his own. However, just knowing all would be safe from the king's tyranny made all the other things so worthwhile.

"If I had to do again, I would do nothing differently. I would still do what I am doing now so that all would live and live on. Even with you birds, I would do just what I have done to keep my kingdom here." The eagle asked her if she'd been happy. "Happy? I don't know that I have had that much in my lifetime. I have been content.

Not the same, I suppose, but I have been content with my lot in life. If only I could have kept living the way we have, I do believe I could have made such a difference in things here and in the future. Before I forget this again, I have taken the time to write out the things t'will keep the new town with coin in their coffers. I know it will be aplenty, but I will worry until my last breath if it will be enough."

Her last breath—it was only a few days away. Much too soon for her, but Dante knew it would be well worth the pain of dying. Sitting up, she looked at the birds, all six of them on their perches watching over her and the emptied lands they could see. They were the sole reason she was able to do this. This she knew more than anyone could have guessed.

"I shall retire, I think. I have no bed to speak of now, so I will only lie upon the ticking. On the morrow, we shall have a feast. A great amount of food, as well as drink. 'Tis fitting, I think, to celebrate this new way of life for so many." Her beautiful phoenix asked her why she seemed so sad. "Sad? Aye, I am that and more. Things are moving at a pace I wish didn't exist. But it is for the wellbeing of all that have called this place home. In that, I suppose I am sad that we shall never be able to return here in my lifetime."

But they would. All six of them and more would return someday and see the castle as it should have been, a lovely home to her son and his mate. The one, she herself, had hand-picked for her beloved child. Oh, to be able to see them grow into love. But it was not to be.

Getting up before she made a fool of herself by crying over something she had no control over, Dante did indeed head to her bed. For tomorrow and the next day would be the hardest of anything she'd ever done.

~*~

Dante didn't sleep. She'd not closed her eyes to rest in more years than she could count on both her hands and then her toes. It was all right, she supposed. Dante was able to get more done this way. But she did pace herself. She'd never survive these last days if she were to fall apart now.

"Mistress, there are two men here to see you. They wish to know who has carved your turrets. I did not tell him the birds atop the castle are as real as he." Mary shook her head at the folly of some men. "I should have called them down to talk to him about how they were made. I think he might well have soiled his britches."

"Mary, please tell them the lady of the castle is busy and does not have time to tell him of the art he is looking at. What manner of person would ask such a thing? As if I didn't have the sense of that turtle caught in the drain last week. Nay, tell them to move on before I toss them into the sea."

Mary went to tell them just what she had said. Dante was smiling when she heard Mary laughing. She'd no doubt make the way she'd told her to move them on to extremes. It would serve the men right if she really would call down one of her birds to take care they didn't bother her again.

Dante made her way to the drying room at the back of the kitchen. She had been brewing a brew for several days now.

"You're not going to be going with us, are you, my lady?" She turned to look at her great phoenix. "If you do not explain to me what your plan is, I think to tell your falcon what I have figured out. She will not allow you to die. Nor will I be all right with your death."

"I must die, my beautiful friend. For if the king were to find that this castle and all that was here when he set sail were gone, what do you think he'd say to his men? That it was a good thing she left? That now he didn't have to kill her? Nay, he would send them to find me and my people. I do not wish anyone else to be harmed for what he wants from me." The phoenix, Piper, would be her name someday, asked her if she expected her birds to do the killing of Dante. "In a way. I have this brew here. It is nearly set for me to drink down. The castle and its walls, they must come down, or it will be all for naught. I might have misjudged something in my dream, so I wish to make sure that all is taken care of, including my people. This, what I have made—it will have me dead before you drop the first stone upon the only home I have ever had. You as well, my dear bird, must be gone should he arrive."

"Mercy will not be willing to help." Dante told her she would because she'd know what Dante said now was the truth. "Aye, you say that, but I think her to be most upset with the turn of events, my lady. It will break all our hearts to know you have left us behind."

"I shall never leave any of you behind. I will be forever in your hearts, and you in mine as I take my last breath." The phoenix nodded but didn't say anything more for some time. "He will die before he gets to the land. This king who thinks to murder me in my own bed. And those that he brought with him, they too will perish. 'Tis a folly on his part to think I'd just do as he wants as if I have no mind of my own. I know Mercy will kill him and all that have been forced to come here with him. It's not such a bad thing, these deaths, Phoenix. It will be merciful to all that have ridden the seas to make their way here."

After the bird left her, she pulled the large cauldron off the hot flames and covered it with a lid. Even though there were no children about nor anyone working in the kitchens, she would feel terrible if any harm would come to anything right now. Making her way back to the throne room, or what was left of it, she laid on the floor to look up at the sky.

Dante hated heights. While she forever knew she'd never see the time when there would be airplanes in her sky, she knew they were set to come. She was content, for now, to bask in the beautiful view she'd miss more than she thought she might.

Getting up, Dante made her way to the side of the castle that faced the sea.

"Oh, to see the waterways filled with my own ships again. To see them sailing off to find new things to bring back to us." There were ships out there—she could just make out their flags. None of these were her tormentor, she knew. He would be visible in two days. Still a long way out to sea. He would be nothing more than a small speck in the open waters, but she'd still be able to see him. "Why now? Why have you made your plans to include me at this time? I wish more and more I'd been born a male. Then no one would dare to come here. I might well have been the king of all the lands had it been so."

Her ships had been taken to the coves not far from here. By the time they were remembered, they would be nothing more than rotted wood and material. Dante wouldn't want them to be seaworthy again. It might well be the thing that got her people killed. Even in the future, the bits and pieces she could see, the ships would only cause people to look harder for her remains and perhaps run into New Town, where her people lived. That, she knew, would be a danger to all.

"Mother? Are you here?" She turned to look at her son. Duncan had been coming to her of late to get more lessons and her thoughts on things, as well as how to manage a vast kingdom such as the one she was leaving him. "I thought for sure you'd be here. I have a favor to ask of you. 'Tis a small one, but one I think you can give me. I should like to spend the night here, within these walls, once with you. I have spoken to Mary about it, and she thinks you will grant me this one wish. It will be the first and last time the two of us will be able to be under the same roof since I was born."

"I should like that. Very much." He nodded and smiled at her. "There is so much to tell you, and so much more, I think I have forgotten to pass on to you. But for this night, I shall not speak of the king coming here. Nor of my life ending. You are aware of it, my child. This, I know. But to have you here with me this last night? It is more than I could have asked for."

They made their plans to sleep on the same ticking she'd been resting on since her bed had been taken away. As they curled up under a thick blanket, the two of them talked more than they rested. Tears were shed, of course. There was no way to avoid such a thing. But there was laughter too, much more of it than tears.

"I shan't be here tomorrow when you are set. I cannot be of sound mind when I know what is to happen to you. I will tell you, Mother, that there couldn't have been a better person to raise me. Nor one that has loved me as well as you have." She kissed him on the forehead as he spoke again. "For so long as I live, Mother dear, I will keep you in my heart, along with the birds that will be mine as well. I love you—much more than I think any child could their parent. You are the best there is. I shall kill anyone that says differently."

She had no words to give him after that. Her heart, already tender, was breaking more. It might well have done her better not to have spent the night with her son. But it would have been harder on her, she thought, to not have this time with him with no others around.

Finally, when she could speak without tearing up, even more, Dante told her son that she loved him. That he'd be a better king than she had been a queen. After saying that, they both settled into their thoughts until the sun came rising up from the seas that surrounded them.

Today, she knew, would be her last day to breathe in the air and take in food for her belly, and the very last time she'd order her birds to do something she knew they'd hate her for.

# *Chapter 1*

Glad that the holidays were over, Piper resigned herself to the fact that she would still have to travel a great deal, as well as work. It wasn't that she was getting bored with what she was doing—she loved making art from pieces of metal and other things more than she did most of the things she'd done in her life. What she was having issues with was twofold. She didn't want to work, and she didn't want to travel.

"You don't have to do either. I know you're well aware of that." Piper glared at her sister Remi. "Well, you don't. Just take some time off and do nothing for a while. You'd be surprised at how invigorating it can be."

"Oh yeah? When was the last time you took time off to lay about? I can tell you. Never. You're a bigger workaholic than I am." She looked at the piece she was working on. It was going to be beautiful if she did say so herself. However, that wasn't the issue, either. "I'm not bored, but I hate doing things that people want. Why can't they just purchase the things I like and leave me alone? I want to make a phoenix again, this one larger than life. I want to work on this project instead of putting things together that people want to show off. Damn it, I want my stuff to be just that. Mine."

"What is it you're making now anyway? I'm sorry, but I can't see the end product in this one." She pointed to the wall where the plans were. Piper hadn't been one for plans before. But with the help of Joel and him engineering what she wanted the end product to look like, she didn't have so many failed attempts as she had before. Actually, she'd not had a single one fail. Joel seemed to understand her babbling about what she needed him to work out for her. "This is beautiful, Piper. And the fact that it's your design that makes it all the more special. What are you going to do with it once you have it finished?"

The castle. She had laid in her bed with her eyes closed as the entire thing came together in her mind one night. Not only what she was making, but also the colors that would be put into it. She would use their feathers. For each of the birds that would be atop the castle, a single feather would be used to make them true to life in color, as well as to show off their size. There was no doubt in her mind that she'd never get enough money for it to want to sell it. It was for her and her alone.

It occurred to her sometime later that she was alone in her studio. There were still the little people that lived in the building with her. They would come down after everyone was gone for the evening and clean up her mess. Not that there was ever much to do, but it would be like she'd never blown flames over metal where shavings of it would fall. Nor would her empty bottles of water and empty bags of seeds be lying about either.

In favor of working on the castle, she worked on the falcon, Mercy's bird of prey. The feather she'd asked for a week ago from each of them had done just what she'd hoped. It looked like the big bird had simply landed on her table and had hardened. Piper only hoped the others would go so well.

"Aunt Piper?" She looked up from the piece she was working on. Piper was her big bird, the only way she could get the heat she needed. However, it didn't seem to bother the child in front of her. It took her befuddled mind a few seconds to realize who it was. "It's Abe Dante. I wanted to talk to you if you'd not mind. But I can come back if this isn't a good time."

She shifted back from her bird and sat down. It had startled her, she thought. So involved in her work, she'd completely forgotten where she was, as well as that there might be others in the room with her.

"I'm sorry." He turned away from her. "No. Don't go, Abe. I'm sorry I was so wrapped up in what I was doing that— Well, you must have said my name more than once, I'm thinking."

"Yes. But I was watching you work too. I've never seen you working before." He smiled at her, and she knew right then that this kid was going to be a heartbreaker. "You're all sweaty. I'll get you a bottle of water."

"What time is it?" He told her as he moved to the fridge that was magically filled with water just for her. "My goodness. Six o'clock? Sheesh. I never realized— obviously. How about I take my favorite guy out to dinner for keeping me from working through the night?"

"You mean me?" She nodded at him as he brought her a drink. "Sure. That would be fantastic. Then I can ask you something. I have to ask my mom and dad first. They're working late tonight. I told them I was going to come here and see you."

"Good. Never take off from anywhere without telling someone. Being the prince of a castle might make people stupid enough to try and hurt you. Then they'd be dead." All the kids had been talked to over the last few weeks. "Where would you like to go?"

"I can pay if we go someplace like burgers. I have money now, but I'm learning to make sure I don't spend it willy nilly. Grandpa told me it's good to have money, but if you're stupid with it, you'll be as broke as you were rich. I love that guy." She nearly told him she'd pay but saw the look on his face. "I can pay, Aunt Piper. Besides, this will make me feel better about asking a favor of you."

She drove them to the hamburger place, driving like

she was an old woman most of the way. Piper had great skills at driving fast. Being a racecar driver for a while had shown her moves that she had fun with. But the first time she took a curve today going well over the speed limit, she glanced over at Abe and realized she was scaring the shit out of him. Slowing down had him also stop white knuckling the door handle.

After they ordered and Abe paid, they sat at one of the many empty tables. Piper watched him as he meticulously set his hamburger on the open wrapper, smack dab in the middle. After getting that set up, he dumped his fries onto the wrapper and made sure they were arranged by size, largest to smallest. Opening just one ketchup tube, he picked up the largest fry, and after dipping it in the perfect red circle of the sauce, he ate it in small bites. He looked at her when she laughed.

"Has anyone pointed out to you that you're OCD? Not that it's a bad thing, but you really should try to lighten up a little, kid. People will think you're odd." He told her that most already did. "I love you, anyway. And I'm glad you asked me out."

"Me too. I have to retake my tests for school tomorrow. Mom probably told you I didn't do what I should have on the first one." Piper told him Jude had told her. "Not that I failed, but I didn't want anyone to think I was smart. Tracy was a little upset with me for thinking she of all people would care."

"She's right, you know." He nodded as he ate all his

fries before starting on the burger. "Do you ever just mix up what you're eating? I mean, do you eat a fry then a bite of burger?"

"No. That would be wrong." He grinned at her. "I'm just funning with you. I do like order, but not in my food. It's just me trying to be funny."

"You had me hooked. That's a good one." She finished off her burger and decided she'd get more food when she got home. She didn't want to break the bank for him and him not coming to see her anymore. "All right. What is this favor you need from me?"

"I took the school test last week. I tested out of everything they gave me. Now I have to go to the college to see how much I can test out of there. Mom seems to think I should just take my time in college classes. Not to take a lot so I can ease into this. Dad said I should go for it." Piper didn't know where this was going, but she was extremely proud of this kid. "Anyway, I was wondering if you'd help me with an art project I have to put together so I can test out of the art classes they're giving me."

"Okay. I have no idea what you're talking about. You sort of went around the bush about forty times. Just tell me what you're kind of not telling me." He told her he was nervous. "Of me? I'm not going to harm you, kid. I love you."

"I love you too. All right. Let me think." She went to get herself three more burgers and a malt. While she was there, keeping an eye on Abe, she ordered him another burger, as well as a malt. When she sat back down with him, he said he thought he had it. "I'm having trouble fitting in with people my own age. I think that's why I was so excited to get tested out of high school and being with kids that are more on my level. But that's not working out so well. The older kids treat me worse than the others do. Not that they're hurting me, but I guess no matter where I go, I'm going to have people making fun of me. Anyway. There is a college for gifted people. I'm not saying I'm gifted, but I like to read. They want to see some work I can do. I've not told Mom and Dad about this school yet. I know it's really expensive, but I think I'll like it there better than any other place I've been."

"What's the name of the college?" He told her. "Okay. Just so you know, your mom and Aunt Mercy have a lot to do with that college. They donate every year to their fundraisers. So that might be an in for you. What else do you have to do for them to be accepted?"

"An outstanding art project. Know two languages. I have to show them I'm able to read on a higher level than twice my age. Then I have to be able to be on some of the teams. I'm not sure what that might be, but I think it's like debate teams or something." She told him they had competitions yearly for scholarships. Debates were only a small part of it. "I didn't know that, but I think I can hold my own so long as I don't have to be in any sports. I love to watch football and other contact sports, but I'm too little for much more than watching."

"You'll grow into it. So, you need me to help you with the outstanding art project. What did you have in mind? And so you know, I'm not going to do it for you." He said he'd hoped she wouldn't. "What did you have in mind?"

He told her how he was thinking of making a map of the United States in relief format. "I know you worked with all kinds of media before you came to blowing heat. I was wondering if you'd show me how to make clay work for what I have in mind. I don't want you to do it for me, but to show me how to work with the clay so I can figure out what I'm doing."

"I can do that. On one condition." He nodded and said he had to tell his parents. "That's right. I won't mind helping you, kid, but I'm not going behind their backs to do that. We're very close, and I'd hate for any one of them to be upset with either of us."

"I understand. The reason I went to you first was to make sure I could get some help with the projects. The others are easy enough for me. I've been looking around in the books Grandma Dante left for you guys, and Latin isn't easy, but I'm learning it. Also, I have a program on my computer that is teaching me Spanish. It's fun."

"Most people wouldn't think learning Latin is fun, buddy. It's a difficult language for most people." He grinned at her. "Everything else you have on this list you told me about, you have it down pat too, I'm assuming."

"Yes. I've been reading since I was living with my

other parents. I could work with numbers too. That was one of the things that got me into trouble when they had me. Even as a little kid, I was smarter than they were." He looked around the restaurant and then back at her. "I'm afraid, Aunt Piper. I'm so afraid they'll know where I am and who's adopted me and come back for me. I have this feeling they're not only out there looking for me, but they'll take me too."

"Have you heard from them in any way?" He said he'd not, that he was probably being silly. "You're magical, Abe. I know you're aware of that. If you think this, feel it, then I'd think you have the right idea about them. Tell me what you know about them."

He handed her a copy of his birth certificate. She had a feeling he'd gone online and ordered it for himself. She read the two names there and felt the hair at her neck tingle. Putting it away by sending it to her home, she looked at the kid.

"I have two questions for you. You have to be honest with me about it, all right?" He told her he'd never lie to any of them. "Good. The first question. Do you know how you ended up in the home in the first place? What I mean is, did they take you there or was it someone else?"

"The police. I guess they dropped me off at the hospital. I'd been hurt by my parents, so they'd have a reason for wanting me there. Then they left. The police took me to the home that night. That's where I met Tracy." She nodded and thought about the second question.

"Ask me. I can take it."

"You were sexually abused at the home. Did you... were you abused at home with your parents?" He said no. No hesitation, just a simple no. "How were you hurt when they dropped you off?"

Abe stood up and pulled his sleeve to his shirt to his elbow. The mark there made her think the fucking shits had burned him. However, when she touched it, Piper saw just what had happened to have scarred the kid for life.

"What do you want me to do?" He sat back down, and she watched his face. He wasn't as readable as she had hoped he'd be. When he put his hands on the table, laying his over hers, she braced herself for whatever he was about to say to her. "Tell me, Abe."

"Dead. I want them dead." He squeezed her hands. "I know you can do it. I know you and the other birds have killed before. They're not going to stop, I don't think, until they have me dead. I know I can't die, but I was told I could be mutilated in a way that would be forever. Like blinded. They cut off my hand or something. They'll also try and hurt Mom and Dad. Tracy too. I don't want them to come here at all."

Piper told him she'd talk to him later about what he wanted. After that, the two of them talked about the clay and how to work it. She was sure that whatever else they'd done to him, it was going to be far worse than anyone had thought. Piper was afraid to look and see what she could learn about his biological parents.

When she took him home, Piper was glad to see the others were at the castle. After Abe said he needed to work on something, he left them in the living room. Piper stood up and started to pace. Telling them what she'd learned tonight was difficult to share. It wasn't breaking a promise to him—he'd told her she could talk to the others. But it was going to hurt Duncan and Jude a great deal, she thought.

"I've had a long conversation with Abe. There are things he told me, things I'm sure you've not been aware of. Mostly it has to do with his parents." Piper looked at Mercy. "You need to find them. Now. He believes they're on their way here."

"They are. That's why we're here tonight to figure out what to do about it. Since Christmas, I've had a couple of people keeping an eye on them. They're making their way here to reclaim their son." Piper asked her where they were. "They're having difficulties that are keeping them from arriving too soon. What is it you know that we should?"

"Abe wants them dead." No one said a word for several minutes. "He's terrified they're going to try and take him and then harm you guys. I didn't tell him they were coming; he knew they were. I think, like Dante, he can see bits of the future."

~*~

Abe waited in line to purchase the map he was going

to work from. After reading the instructions through twice, he knew he could use a purchased map to start his project, but he had to make it wholly his. Excitement ran over his body as he was next in line to buy what he needed.

The little store wasn't busy. It was one of the new shops that had opened in town a few weeks ago—an art supply store that had everything a person could want to work on something fun. He'd been tempted to buy himself some of the paints that were on the shelf, but he didn't want to be distracted from what he was doing now. Maybe later, he told himself.

Then he saw the woman coming into the store with a big man. As they walked by him, Abe was pushed back a few feet. Neither of them said a word to him, but Abe knew they were in here for trouble. He did the only thing he could think of and reached out to his dad. He knew he was in town today for several meetings. Mom was looking for some plants to put around the house.

*I'm at Arts and Crafts.* Dad asked him if he was short on money. *No. I have enough. There are two people in here that have plans to kill the woman that is ringing us out.*

*Do you see any guns?* Abe told him they didn't have any. They were going to cut her up with the knives they had on them. *What will happen to the others in the store, son? I'm on my way there with Joel.*

*There won't be any of us in here. They're waiting on all of us to leave. Dad, I'm the last person in line. I think the three people ahead of me are together, so when they leave, it'll just be me and them.* Dad told him that they were nearly there. *All right. I'm not afraid. I just don't want Mrs. Clarity hurt.*

Joel entered the store first. He looked at him and winked, then asked if he had everything he needed. It wasn't until he was ushered out of the building that he realized what Dad was doing—getting Abe out of harm's way as well. Dad told him to go get the police and to stay there. Running down the sidewalk, he forgot to tell them to be careful.

The police were still talking on and on about leaving the station, and Abe wanted to beat them up. They were taking their time about going to help his dad. When it looked to him like they weren't ever going to get going, he called for his mom and the others. He was sure the next time he needed extra help, the police weren't going to be called. They weren't taking it seriously at all.

When the man was brought into the station where Abe was, he was mad. Not only had the police only just left the station, but his family had been the ones that had stopped the violence in the shop. He wanted to say something to the officers, but he was afraid he'd be in trouble. However, his dad had no such problems and told them off. Then he fired them.

"I'd rather know my family is safe because of the response from the police than think that my wife and her sisters needed to be called in for back up." The chief said they'd not believed the kid. "That *kid* is my son. And it shouldn't have mattered one bit that he came to you to tell you about what was going on. It should have had you out the door as fast as you could be."

Hiring a new set of policemen wasn't nearly as difficult as he thought it might be. Dad not only had a new crew in place shortly but more of them than before. The man in charge of the station now was someone he knew. Mr. Pilgrim was teaching him to tell the difference between shifters and humans at the packhouse. He asked Dad what had happened at the shop.

"Mrs. Clarity had had some issues with her daughter and son-in-law before, but usually they'd just rob her then take off. After she opened her shop, they'd been hanging around more. When she wouldn't give them any cash, they decided they'd kill her. Great family there, I think." Dad looked at him as he continued. "I'm going to have to have Abe here tell you how he knew. But it's not to go any further than this room."

"I think I know. He's got some kind of magic that tells him what's going on. He's been displaying it at my house for the last few weeks." Dad asked him what he'd done. Abe was curious too. "Mae, my little girl, was playing on the floor, minding her toys when Abe there jumped up and took one of the blocks from her. He said she was going to swallow it. Not that she could or might, but that she was going to. There were other things too. Like he grabbed a cup just as it was crashing to the floor. He was in the living room when he rushed in and caught the cup as it tumbled off the table I'd hit with my body. I figured he was either seeing things that were gonna happen, or he was just one lucky kid."

"I have to touch someone to know what's going on." Dad got down to his level and asked him if he'd seen what they did to Mrs. Clarity. "Yes."

Dad only looked at him for a few seconds before he nodded. Abe was glad he didn't ask more. He didn't want to have to explain to him how terribly bad they'd cut her up. She was a really nice person.

Uncle Joel had gotten his map for him as well as the paints he'd wanted. He told him that Mrs. Clarity had seen him eyeing them, and she wanted him to have them. He felt bad that she'd given them to him, but Dad told him to take them, as she was grateful to be alive, and that made her feel better. So he went home with his dad and family to start on his project.

He had talked to them last night about the college. Abe had really thought they'd be mad at him for doing things behind their backs, but all they said was, it was good. That doing research on the college had been the right move. Knowing about the place made them think he was serious about attending as well. Abe told them that Aunt Piper was going to show him a few things about clay usage.

Now, here he was working on his project on the dining room table. Abe was having fun with it and was excited to see it come together. Mostly, he thought, he wanted to show his parents that he was very serious about this school and hoped he'd be able to get in on his own without having his mom telling them to take him. She said she could do that for him and would be glad to do it.

"I'd rather do it on my own. So I can feel good about it." She told him she understood that. "I've got to make sure I can stand up on my own two feet rather than have to fall back because I let you get me in. Does that make sense?"

"It does. You want to feel good about your education rather than worry about you only succeeding because I pulled a few strings for you." He nodded. "Good for you. But know this—if you need me to step in for you, for anything, then you only need to let me know. I'm your mom, and no one is going to hurt you so long as I live."

"Thanks, Mom. I love you too."

Abe did love them, every one of the birds and their mates. He figured that soon they'd all have mates and babies on the way, and there would be that many more people he could call his own. So long as his bio parents, what Tracy called them, were not in the picture.

Last night before he'd gone to bed, he did that reaching thing. He could contact anyone in his family and figured he might be able to tell where the bios were. The only time he'd felt them was a few weeks ago. Something about them had called out to him. Abe had figured out later that it was them saying his name. Nothing more, just them talking about him. Trying it again now, he could actually see what they were doing.

His bio mom was Retha. But she spelled it wrong so people would remember her. Like anyone could forget her blue hair and tatted up face. "Did you think about what happens if they don't want him anymore? I mean, we're planning on taking him then selling him back. But what if they just say we can have him? I don't want him around, Tag. Just the money."

Tag. He supposed his bio father's name would have been shortened to Tag from Taggert. "Have you figured out how much he's going to be worth yet?"

"No. I'm still working on where he's at. The newspaper talking about some king getting married and adopting two kids only said that they were in upper Ohio. That don't tell me much." Bio mom looked around. "Do you ever feel like someone is watching us? I mean, like right here in the room with us?"

"I don't feel that. Maybe it's you not being high yet that has you feeling that way. Come on, share what you have." Drugs. That was when Abe noticed they were tying off a rubber thing around their arms. He moved back away from them but returned when Tag spoke again. "We could just take him and sell him on the black market again. It worked out okay for us then. I don't like how that ended, though. Those people that bought him off us, they turned him over to the cops. That was shitty of them if you ask me."

Now he knew how he'd ended up in the home. They'd sold him. Thinking about that made him realize they were no better than the woman at the home. Worse, he thought, because he had been their son. As he made his way to bed that night, he thought about what he'd said to Aunt Piper. He did wonder if this would make a difference to them if he told them. Abe was going to tell his mom first. She might have a better plan for them. He didn't care, just so long as they never came around him.

Falling asleep was easier since living here. He didn't wake in the middle of the night, terrified that he was going to be murdered in his bed. Abe had witnessed it once. The man that had taken one of the older kids had snapped his neck while his sister stood there, telling him to hurry before anyone woke up. Abe hadn't eaten the cookies that came with dinner that night and figured it was the reason he wasn't sleeping. The cookies had something in them. Abe never ate another cookie while there. He couldn't even stand them now that he knew no one was going to kill anyone in the night. They were off the list of foods he enjoyed.

# Chapter 2

Grant remembered the birds from when he'd been in the castle keep. They were something to behold, he remembered. He also remembered the old king. The fucking bastard had nearly killed his mother when she'd been in labor with him. It was small wonder either of them had survived working there.

Today he was digging a trough from the waterway to the back of his home. Grant had his mom move in with him some years ago. It was still the same now. They worked well together and didn't have the problems with being together, as did some of the humans he knew living with their parents. He supposed it was because they were both magical and could make walls between them if they wanted some quiet time. Not that he wanted much of that anymore. He seemed to love being around groups more than he did when he'd been younger. Grant supposed it was because of his job as a doctor. That was his latest job anyway.

"Are you going to go with me to the castle in the morning?" Grant ask his mom why she was going there. "The lady of the house wants me to come by there and see if I can do anything with the material that was left in the castle for them. There are a few tapestries as well that she thinks could use a steady hand. To think the birds are all back now. It's nice, don't you think?"

"Yes." He didn't really care if they were back or not. He'd not had a great deal to do with them when he'd been here long ago and didn't figure that was going to change all that much now that they lived around him. "I'll have this dug out for you in an hour. Will you be ready to set up the water system for your herbs by then?"

His mom was the healer. Grant knew she also used magic when she made herbs or the like to help people. Being a fae, she was in tune with the earth more than most. Mostly she only made wraps or helped birth a baby or two. But she knew everyone in town, and they'd been using her forever, it seemed.

As soon as he had the water running the way she wanted it, it was easy for her to hook up the sprinkler system to turn on the herbs when she wanted. Grant laughed when she stood under the spray of water and cooled off.

"I think this summer is going to be a hot one." He didn't tell her the very definition of summer meant it would be hot, but he kept his mouth closed. "Do you suppose there is a chance we can get a few trees back here trimmed back? I'm tired of picking up sticks when the wind blows a little harder than usual."

"I can do that. How far do you want them trimmed? I'm assuming you mean higher and not just trimmed off the fence." She told him what she wanted. "All right, Mom. I can do that for you. But you're about to have company. The ground is telling me it's a child because of the light foot. Male too."

"Oh, I forgot. It's Abe from the castle. He was coming by for some information on some herbs. I have them ready." She started for the house and stopped. "Grant, they're on the table laid out for him. Could you go in and hand them to him? I'm soaked through right now."

He didn't mind. Grant had seen the kids around town a few times. He'd also heard that Abe had saved one of the merchants the other day. He wanted to thank him for that, as well as invite him to his classes about surviving in the wild. Grant thought everyone should be able to tell a weed from something they could eat to stay alive.

"You must be Mr. Grant." He said he was just Grant. "All right, Grant. I'm Abe. Your mom, she said she had some starters she could give me for a project." He told him to come into the house, and he'd get them. "This is so cool. It's so big here."

The house, like a great many of the houses here, was smallish. The difference was, with their home, it only looked like it was small from the outside. The inside of his home was much larger and spacious than the biggest home here because of their magic.

"When I first was moved into this home with my mom, we both knew it was never going to hold us both and all our projects. So we worked out what we wanted and made our own space. Usually, the magic doesn't show itself to others. You must be very trustworthy." Abe told him he hoped so. "I was going to ask you if you'd like to come to the survival classes I'm working on. I think your sister and cousin might enjoy them as well. I teach you how to know what you can do if you're lost."

"I'd have to ask my mom and dad." Grant handed him permission slips to give them. "I'll drop one of them off with Miley when I see her. She's supposed to come to the house for dinner tonight anyway. You should come too. That way, if they have any questions, you'll be able to answer. It will be fun to have someone other than all those women around."

"I don't know, kid. What if they don't want strangers around?" Abe said he wasn't a stranger, that he knew his sister and mom both. "But they still might not like it. You should probably get permission first for me to just show up."

He nodded then smiled at him. "I asked. Mom said the more, the merrier, and that your mom should come too. Tracy had so much fun at your mom's shop the other day that she has talked of nothing much else. Please say you're coming. I will have someone to talk to while the women talk about dresses and stuff." He made a gagging sound, then looked up at Grant. "It's not that bad. I promise. I love having all my family around all the time. Especially at meal times. They're fun."

"I have to ask my mom too." Abe told him if she couldn't make it, he could still come. "You're an all right kid. I think I might like having you hanging around with me."

"My Aunt Piper calls me kid too. I don't think it's because she doesn't know my name, but she just thinks of me as a kid. I don't annoy her, I don't think. We had dinner together the other night. Just her and me." The kid had a serious crush on his aunt if Grant didn't miss his bet. "She's the phoenix. The scariest of all of them, I think. My mom is an eagle. So is Dad."

In the end, it was just him that was going to dinner at the castle. His mom wanted to go, he could tell, but she'd already made plans to go over to Ms. Sanders' home and help her with her legs. Abe told her that if she got done early to come on up. He'd love to have her sitting with them too. The kid was a charmer. He could tell that right away.

When it was time for him to head up to dinner, his mom actually going, after all, he thought about what he should wear. When he came out of his room in a pair of jeans and a white shirt and tie, his mom fussed at him for not dressing up more.

"Mom, if he would have told me to dress more, I would have. But he said they just wore what they had on. Just in case he was a little too casual about the dress, I'm wearing a tie." She told him he needed to shave. Also that his hair was too long. "Mom, you being nervous isn't helping me much, just so you know."

"I don't want to make a terrible impression." He pointed out that they'd met them before. "I know, but we were working. That's different."

Rolling his eyes, he went out onto the porch to wait for her to come out so they could leave. Getting into the car for the short drive, Grant knew they'd be stopped several times before they made it out of the town, and that would delay them a great deal.

As they made their way to the castle, talking to their neighbors as they went, Grant realized how much his mom meant to these people. He would also bet his mom would tell him they were just being nice. No, he thought, they loved her. As much as he did. His mom was the best there was as far as he was concerned.

Grant also knew people would come to her about things too. Her opinion meant a great deal to each and every one of the townspeople. Even the mayor came to her about things he wasn't sure were going to work. Grant had to laugh. He knew she'd have an opinion about whatever it was.

"Oh, my goodness." He looked where his mom was

looking and stopped the car. The castle was finished. The scaffolding had been taken down sometime over the last few days. In addition, the drawbridge, as old as the castle itself, had been installed. "It looks so much like it did when you were born, Grant. With the exception of the dirt and smoke."

"The smell too. It doesn't smell of pigs or sewage." She nodded as she stared at the place. "Mom? Are you ready to go on?"

"Aye, I am. My goodness, the queen would surely be proud of her boy. Not just in taking care that the castle was restored, but how all of us are still here, as safe as the day she had us moved." She laughed a little and turned to him while he still had the car in park. "You were so sick on that trip we took. If not for everything going on down below us, you might well have not spewed your breakfast and lunch."

"Yes. You kept telling me not to look down. But I'd never been that high before." He thought of that day, and it still terrified him to think just how high they had been. "If I remember correctly, the bird that took us was the owl. She was as gentle as she could be, too, I remember."

He thought of all the changes that had occurred in his lifetime. There wasn't a day that went by that something new wasn't discovered. A patch of land that was quickly turned into one of the best herb gardens ever. Everyone kept it cleaned of weeds, and it was used by all. The running stream that seemed to be warmer in the colder months. He remembered taking baths in the stream with a great many other boys his age. Each house had water piped in. Wood used for cooking and heat was chopped and stacked in the summer and used up through the winter. Any need they were lacking in did not matter either. Someone was there to work out a solution. When one of their own died, they all worked together to take care of the family left behind. The casket would be made for them as well.

When they pulled up in front of the castle, Grant wondered what would have happened to them had not the queen of the castle provided for them. Even now, she had made sure there was plenty to go around. He thought that if Dante were alive today, she'd be working the fields with them if necessary. She'd be helping dig graves, a new well or whatever was necessary.

While he'd never met her person to person, everyone knew who she was. It was nothing, when they were all living in the keep, for her to be seen grooming horses or playing with the children she came across. Also, she'd be the first to go to a home that had a dying relative, holding their hands when grief would be too much for them.

"I wish I could have known her." He looked around when someone said she did as well. "You must be Tracy. I've heard a great deal about the beautiful teenagers here now. How do you like living in a castle?"

"It's wonderful. You must be Grant. Your mom told one of us to come out and get you. She seems to think you're off your noodle. I myself think that if anyone can stop and enjoy a beautiful scene such as this one, there can't be too much wrong with them." He looked back out over the inlet. There were boats on the water even now. "Someday, I'd like to be able to ride the seas. My mom did. She said that being a pirate with her sisters was one of the most fun times she can remember."

"I would imagine." He thought about this young slip of a woman being a pirate. "I bet in her day it was very profitable too. Men would have gladly turned over anything to a pretty face. I was a pirate, too, for a while. For me, it was a good way to make some money to send home to my mom. It certainly did stave off the boredom for a while."

They talked about his stint as a pirate. Also, when he'd been other things in his life. As soon as he entered the large double doors, Grant felt warmed. Not by the room, but by the feelings that came from it. The part of him that was fae told him this would be a good place to feel welcomed no matter what sort of day you were having.

Grant bowed to the woman he knew to be his queen.

"Oh, please don't do that. I nearly had to kick your mother up from the floor when she did the same thing. Get up." He did and grinned at the pretty woman in front of him. "I might be your queen and Duncan, your king, but as friends, as I'm hoping you'll be, we're just people having friends over for dinner."

"I doubt very much that you'll get my mom to do anything but bow or curtsy in front of you." Jude, he'd been asked to call her, laughed. "You've done so much to the castle. I could swear that other than a few things, such as smell, you've done it exactly as it was all those centuries ago."

"Yes. I remember the smell." She laughed with him. "Isn't it funny how you can remember a lot of good things about a place, but when someone brings up the bad part, it floods your memory with all sorts of other things? Like the smell of cooking meat. The smokehouse too. My goodness. I'd forgotten about those. Dante did try and make it cleaner, but there wasn't the sort of equipment we have now. Come in, Grant. Your mom is now trying to have a conversation with my husband, and I don't think it's going well."

He was led to a large living room space. Whoever had designed it had taken into account that many people might gather in the room. Three massive couches faced the now cooled fireplace. The armor around it gave testament to the wars that had been fought. There were chairs set about in pairs with small tables between them. He found his mom in one of those little areas, trying her best to blend into the chair while sitting across from Duncan, their king.

"Your mother seems to think she is beneath me, Grant. I'm trying to tell her I don't recognize such stations in life anymore. I can and will be king when it's necessary, but we're friends here today." Grant shook hands with the other man and felt a surge of magic transferred between the two of them. "Ah. Fae, faerie, and brownie. I think there is a bit of wolf there as well. As well as a little magic from my mom. I've read about you, Grant. My mother had such plans for you."

"I'm sorry. What?"

Duncan just laughed and turned when three women came into the room with them. They were beautiful beyond compare, but Grant thought all women were beautiful. Once he was introduced to them, shaking all their offered hands, he started to join his mom. She'd taken the opportunity to escape from the chair she'd been in and move to the couch.

When Duncan cleared his throat, Grant looked to where he was looking.

"Holy Christ."

~*~

Piper stared at the man who was staring so intently at her. "I have to go as soon as we're finished with dinner." Taking her eyes off the man while she looked at Duncan was harder than she thought it should have been. "There was an explosion in Kentucky. They're saying it is larger than the one they had back in seventy-seven at the supper club."

"I remember that. There were a lot of people killed there because of something to do with doors." She said they'd not opened in the way that was now law. Duncan told her the name of the place. "The fire broke out in the kitchen, and when people rushed to the doors, they were crushed because they couldn't pull the doors to open inward due to the crush of people behind them."

"Yes. That's it. Over a hundred and fifty people were killed. More were injured. The man that called me to come to the fire said this one is worse. That there might be as many as three hundred dead. I have to head there right after dinner. I'll probably be gone for a few days." Duncan introduced her to the man. "Hello."

Piper wanted to back away from him. Not that she thought he'd harm her, but she had a feeling she wasn't going to like it when he touched her. When he left his hand out there, she had no choice but to shake it. The power surge that ran over her body had her falling back on the floor, the same for Grant. When he sat up, his nose was bleeding, as well as his lip. But he didn't move anymore after sitting there.

"Mom knew the two of you would be mates." Taking her eyes off Grant to look at Duncan, Piper wanted to tell him to shut the fuck up for a minute. "She said that great things would come from this union. As well as great power."

"I don't know what to think about any of this." Grant agreed with her. "I'm not going to be all sappy around you either. I will nip that shit in the bud if you try it. I'm not a romantic type, and I don't want you fawning all over me either. It's gross."

"Since we've only just met, I'm thinking you can take it down a notch or two. My head is spinning from being knocked on my ass, and I have a headache that beats all." Grant stood up. "I'd like to say I'm happy to meet you, Piper, but so far, all you've done is tell me what you're not going to do. Do you have the slightest bit of happiness about finding me?"

"I don't know." Piper looked at her sisters, then back at Grant. "I don't know what to think, to be honest with you. I have so many questions right now that I don't even know where to begin. I'm sorry I snapped at you."

"Thank you for that." He put out his hand and asked her if he could help her up. "I don't know how the power we felt from each other has changed us, but I think I'm even more than I was before. Fae, for the most part. A little of other things as well."

Piper took his hand. Standing up, she was startled by how tall he was. He had to be over six and a half feet tall. She, in her bare feet, was six-two. Not letting go of his hand right away, she looked into his eyes. They were almost a clear blue — icy, she thought. Taking a step back from him, she felt the warmth of him leave her too. Piper was tempted to move closer to him again but decided there were things she needed answers to.

Dinner was called a few minutes later. No one had spoken to her since she'd gotten up from the floor. Not that she thought she could have answered anything asked of her. Her mind was still a mess. She knew some of the things going on in her head were his memories too.

It was just too much for her, and she stood up. But she'd not meant to draw attention to herself and sat back down. Looking down at her plate, her embarrassment making her angry, Piper wanted to take flight right at that minute and never return. But something happened, and her anger as well as her thoughts, seemed to calm a great deal. That was when she noticed that Grant had simply put his hand on her shoulder.

"I'm not being pushy, Piper, but you seemed ready to jump out of your skin." She nodded and thanked him. "No worries there. I'm hoping that when I need it, you can do the same for me."

Piper must have eaten. Her plate had little bits of food on it, and her fork was dirty. However, she couldn't tell anyone, if asked, what it had tasted like. The others around her were talking about the summer plans. All she could think about right now was the man beside her. And what he would expect from her.

Not that any of the other men in their family had done that. All three of the others had been there for her sisters but never made demands on them. It was one of the reasons she loved them so much—they treated their wives like they needed. Soft and pampered at times, but letting them do their own thing when that was necessary. It occurred to her then that Grant was older than her.

"You've been around a long time." He told her he'd been born before the king had taken Dante as his wife. "I didn't know him. I heard a great deal about him. He was a cruel and mean bastard. I don't think I ever even know how he died. I know it wasn't Dante that did it."

"No. She had nothing to do with his death, which I suppose was a good thing. That would have perhaps made the king of the lands come to her sooner. He died in a war, defending his brother's castle. They were both killed the same day. His brother, I don't remember his name at the moment, killed his wife and children when it was obvious he was losing the war. I think that is part of the estate Duncan now owns. As the only living descendant of the brothers, he would have inherited those lands as well."

"It doesn't sound as if his brother was any better than Dante's husband was." Grant said he was right in killing his family. "And how did you come to that conclusion?"

"Had he not taken their lives as he did, quickly and without much in the way of pain, he saved them from being tortured as well as raped. He had two little girls, and they wouldn't have been spared anything that the person that eventually took the castle would have done to them." She said she'd not thought of that. "There wouldn't have been anyone to hide them away either. As you pointed out, he wasn't much different than his brother. He had no loyal people, such as Dante did. Nor did he have much in the way of ships to send them away. When the brother was killed, the people of the land celebrated for days afterwards. Then I think they too were killed when the man who won the castle took over. Dante made sure the lands were seized back for Duncan some years before her death."

She noticed that everyone at the table had gone quiet. Looking at Mercy when she asked for more stories, Piper realized that more than they did, Grant would have a lot of stories about living in the castle before and after Dante. Grant smiled at her when she asked him about the other lands.

"They're still there, as far as I know. I believe they abut this land." Duncan confirmed that it did, and the castle was still intact. "When your father was brought home to be buried, it was thought he'd been killed by his own men. There are still a few of the old guard left in New Town. When I was younger, I would sit with them, and they'd tell me stories of the cruelty of your father. I won't tell them if you'd not like to hear them."

"He was dead before I was born. I know from my mother's books that he wasn't considered a good king. Nor did he stop from putting my mother in her place at times." Grant told Duncan he was sorry for that. "Don't be. There are ways she got around him, mostly because of her magic. But he was a drunkard too. From what I was told, not only did he drink entirely too much, but— my mom's words here—he whored around too. Still, he never had a son by anyone but my mom."

"There were others born to the women he raped. They're all dead now, I believe. I can show you where they're buried if you'd like." Duncan told him he'd like that, then asked Grant what he meant by there being other children. "The women of the castle were raped daily by not just him, but anyone that came to the castle. Three of them and one that lived here had daughters. But they were killed when they were born. The mothers as well. He wanted sons and nothing more. There were no second chances if someone he'd raped had a daughter."

"I didn't know that. I wonder if my mother did." Grant told Duncan she had known about the ones born within the walls. She'd taken care that the families of the murdered were given money. "She never mentioned it in the books. Not even a little bit of that sort of information."

"Something else you might not have known is that we all knew who you were and that your mother was keeping you safe." Duncan looked shocked. Jude asked why no one had said anything. "Dante was good to us all. She never once made any of the people that were hers to protect do anything she'd not do herself. Even going so far as to helping with the dead. We were all loyal to her and only her. Even in her death, she made sure that each and every one of us were able to live out our lives without fear of anyone finding us."

Duncan stood up and asked to be excused. Grant told him he was sorry as he left them there. Looking over at Jude, Piper asked her if he was all right. He did seem to be really upset about the news.

"Yes. He's wonderful, as a matter of fact. These things

you're sharing with us, Grant, are things we might never have known. The very fact that you were around much longer than any of us were gives an insight to Dante and her life that we did not know until now." Jude looked sad herself. "The things she had to endure would have killed a lesser woman, I think. Dante was never perfect, but she was the type of person whose flaws you could ignore because her kindness was so bountiful. We were very lucky to have had someone like her at a time when women were thought of as nothing more than breeding machines. Thank you. From the bottom of my heart, I thank you for sharing. I do hope you'll continue to do so. Oh, welcome to the family, Grant."

After Jude went to check on Duncan, Grant looked at Piper. She was sitting there with her head bowed, and he wondered what she might be thinking. He touched his fingers to her chin and lifted her face up to see her. She'd been crying, and Grant felt his own heart take a tight twist at the sight of so many tears.

"I'm sorry." She shook her head and said it was all right. "Not if I made you cry. I only meant to tell you the stories, and when he asked, I couldn't have turned him down for any reason."

"As Jude said, it's great hearing things that none of us knew. The very fact that you have information she wouldn't have kept in her diary is wonderful news." Piper stood, and so did he. "I have to go. I need to catch the next flight out."

"I'm going." He could tell she wanted to tell him no. "Please? May I go as well? I'd like to be helpful to you if I can. Staying here, without you, I'll not know what to do with myself."

Piper laughed. "I have a feeling you have plenty to do to keep yourself busy. But all right. You can go with me. But you have to do what I tell you. I don't want you hurt any more than I want to be." He said he'd do whatever she told him. "Good. I need to talk to my sisters, then we can leave."

Grant told his mom he'd be back but not to worry. She hugged him several times. Excitement from him having a mate was making her giddy, an emotion he'd never witnessed from his mom before.

Once they were on the plane and in the air, Grant wondered what he would do now that he had a mate. Things, he supposed, would change a great deal for the two of them. How, he wasn't sure, but there would be a lot of laughter and tears before they came together. Smiling to himself, Grant was up for this. He was looking forward to getting to know Piper in any way she'd allow him to. She certainly was a beautiful creature. Grant couldn't wait to see her bird. He had a feeling she was more beautiful than even her human self when she was flying through the sky.

# Chapter 3

Piper had to walk around the area she was in three times before she finally just stepped back and took in a deep breath. She was still standing there with her eyes closed when Grant spoke to her through the link that no one else could breach to find out what was going on.

*I can help you.* She told him she wasn't sure what she was doing, so she didn't know that he could. *I'm fae. I would imagine you are as well now. Or at least partly so. Just dig your fingers into the soot, and you should be able to connect with the land around you. The earth will tell you answers to whatever questions you have.*

*This fire, it was set.* He said he knew that. *Not gasoline. But something just as volatile.*

*It smells to me like burnt grease.* She looked at him as he stood there on the other side of the burnt out building. *I'm not saying that's all I can smell, but I would say it's at least seventy percent of what was used as an accelerant.*

She did as he asked her to do and bent down to the burnt out area she was standing next to. Digging her fingers deep into the debris as well as the dead soil beneath it, she could feel the earth speaking to her just beyond where she was.

*My lady. How may I help you today? I must say I'm glad you are a part of Lord Grant's family. He is a good man. His help with the earth is all that keeps us alive in some areas.* She asked where the fire had started. *Just to the north of you. There you will find what you are searching for. There are others as well, the placements of the cause of the fire. But the item there will show you what you can look for.*

Thanking the earth, giving it a little of her own magic, she felt the shudder of the earth beneath her feet when it thanked her. Moving to where she was told, she sensed Grant coming around the side of the shell that was left and standing by her as she searched for what she'd been told.

"You were right." He said he didn't feel any better about being right. "No. Neither do I, as a matter of fact. But it is grease. She told me there were several more around, but this would help me in what to look for. Do you know if the people have all been accounted for?"

"Two are still missing. But the three hundred dead that they're working with now have all their attention. It's going to be difficult to make sure they're all named. Having the cars on the lot is going to help a great deal."

She knew that, as well. It would help them understand who hadn't left as soon as their meal was over. "I have an idea that I can help with the identification of the dead. If you'd not mind, that is."

"If you can make it so the families can be notified sooner rather than later, that would be wonderful. I think if you can name then, there will be less of a chance that a family member will need to see them looking like they do." She had been in the makeshift morgue twice now. The smell alone was more than she could handle. "The man in charge is Agent Parkerson. He's the one that called me to the scene."

After he left her to find out if he could help, Piper set about finding the other accelerants around the building. It took her six hours to find them all, fearful if she missed anything, it would cause the case to be thrown out of court. The people that had caused this, they needed to be dealt with in the worst possible way.

As night fell on the shell of the building, she found Grant in the makeshift morgue. He had identified the bodies, all of them. It was difficult enough having to go through the place where they had all perished. She could not imagine going through the dead and naming them for their families. Piper found herself a place to rest and to be alone while he finished up. Three hundred and seven people had lost their lives today. The two that had been missing had been found in part of the building, usually left for storage. They'd both been killed as well.

*We have an idea of who caused the fire.* She told Remi she didn't want to deal with anything more today. *I'm sorry, love. I truly am. But you're the only one I can speak with, and you'll need to tell the police.*

*Nearly everyone in this building is dead, Remi. Women and children made up most of the people here today. Please tell me the people who did this are still alive for me to kill.* Remi told her she couldn't do that. *Why not? Who will ever know?*

*The Hillary Corporation will need to be exonerated from this. People will sue them anyway — there are greedy people around everywhere. But if they go under, no one will get paid. The insurance companies need to have someone to blame it on. The owners of the building will also need to have a person they can point to in order to justify paying out so much.* Piper told her all the doors had been locked with chains and locks. *I heard that, as well. The fires were started at each of the exits, so there would be a larger death count. Piper, the five people that did this, they're currently planning another fire to top this one.*

After Remi gave her the information she'd need to tell Parkerson, she went to find him. Her heart was broken for the senseless deaths of the people here. They had come out for a children's event that had been planned for months, only to end up dead.

Grant came to her while she stood telling Parkerson what she knew. Parkerson wrote it all down in his book, then sent his men to the address the people were at. He promised her they'd be in jail before the sun came up.

Grant held her after the agent left her.

"I've never considered myself to be a person who would get their heart hurt over something like this. I'm not saying I'm cold and unfeeling, but the very fact that I have done this for so long sort of jaded me into thinking I've seen it all." Piper looked up at Grant. "They did this for one reason—to have someone speculate on who had done this. How it had been done. They were planning another fire while they were together. That alone makes me want to hunt them down and kill them where they stand."

Grant didn't say anything, but he did continue to hold her. Venting to him, it felt right for some reason. Easier than even screaming at her sisters for what she'd discovered. When she felt him pick her up in his arms, it took her a few seconds to realize she'd fallen asleep standing up. As soon as he sat, she closed her eyes again and let the nightmarish day and night leave her for just a few minutes.

When she woke, she was still in his arms. He was speaking quietly to Parkerson, and she sat up to let them both know that they could speak normally. Grant kissed her on the cheek, then turned her to see Parkerson.

"I was just telling your husband here that the people have been apprehended. They've been taken to the prison for protection. The police station here is already receiving all sorts of death threats to be passed on to them—four women and one man. I nearly had my men make sure they were women before I could let it settle in my head. Women just aren't prone to this sort of thing. Killing children? I never would have believed it." Piper asked him if they'd given any reason for what they'd done. "They did. Just as you were told, they wanted their deeds plastered all over the news. It's a hard thing to wrap your mind around. I can't thank either of you enough for what you've done for us. Without you, this fire might well have been an unsolved case. Not to mention all the dead would still be unidentified."

When Parkerson left them, she moved to the other chair. Piper didn't know what to say to Grant. She wasn't even sure there was anything she could say to him. Thanking him, she thought, and did that. He grinned at her when her belly growled.

"I guess you don't put your hands in your pockets much when you're working." She told him she didn't know. "While you were still looking for the cans of lard, I put some seeds in your pockets. Not a lot, but they would have refilled themselves as you ate. I would have told you, but your mind was such a jumble out there I didn't want to intrude."

Putting her hand into the pocket of the jacket she had on, she pulled it out with a handful of just what he'd told her. Seeds of all sorts of grains were there for her to have been munching on. Eating a handful of them, Piper moaned. Grant laughed.

"Would you like some?" He told her he'd rather have

a steak with all the trimmings. "Me too. I have a card that will feed us both. I've never used it before, but they assure me it's good for whatever I want. I'm sure they mean to feed you as well."

"I'd like that." When he stood up, she did as well. "We're going to have to talk about some things, I think. Mostly try and find out what you've received from me. Also, more of the things that you gave to me. I know now that I can speak with your sisters and brothers. And this is very strange for me, but I can speak with the kids as well. Miley has been telling me your favorite things to do when you're not working too hard."

"She works with us on different projects. Miley, and now the other two, work with us all the time. Tracy has set herself up with a job of delivering food for the elderly, as well as us, when we forget to eat. It happens a good deal more than I'd like to admit." She thought of something as they made their way to the rental they'd picked up. "I was house hunting. I didn't find anything I truly liked yet. Perhaps you can find someplace for us to stay. I've been staying at the castle with the others who haven't been mated as yet. There are only the two of them left, I guess."

"I have a home with my mom, but it's small. It's magical, thanks mostly to us being fae, but it's not nearly large enough for the three of us." She said she understood, then asked if his mom would be living with them. "I hadn't thought of that, but if you'd not mind, I'd like to have her close."

"I'd like for her to be with us too. As you know, I don't have any parents, and the only family I have is the birds and their families." He asked her if she wanted a family. "Someday, yes. We're sort of waiting on Mercy to give birth, which is very soon, to see what sort of baby we might have. I think she's more worried about it than Joel is. He's very laid back."

"I've noticed that about him." Grant laughed as he got behind the wheel to drive them around. "I was also told that you're a terror driving. That you drive like the racecar driver that you once were."

"Abe, right?" He said it was. "Yeah, I sort of had a date with him and just drove like I usually do. When I noticed he was green and might not make it to the restaurant, I did slow down. I don't think he truly relaxed until we were going back to his house later. The kid is super scary smart too."

"Duncan told me he was working on getting into a college for kids like him. I'm to understand he downplayed it at first." Piper said he had. That his biological parents had tossed him away for that very reason. "Did I hear that they might be an issue?"

"You might well have heard it, but we're waiting on them to try to take him from us. Abe wants them dead. He's that afraid of them." Grant pulled into a small brick building's parking lot and asked her if she trusted him. "I do. I guess that's what being mates does, but it's more than that. I don't just trust you, but I feel as if doubting you would be dangerous. Not from you, but some other means. I don't know where that came from, to be honest, but that's what I'm feeling towards you."

"I have the same feelings toward you. By the way, I can shift into a bird too. I've not completely shifted, but while I was in the bathroom earlier, I just thought of being a phoenix, and my hands sprouted feathers. I'm glad I was in there alone. There is no telling what someone might have thought when I screamed like a little kid." He got out and came around to her side of the car. Handing her out, he looked at her when she squeezed his hand. "I've fallen in love with you, Piper. I never thought it really worked like that, but I have to admit, it's a very nice feeling."

"I don't know what I feel about you yet. I like you. You make me feel safe, which is nothing I'd ever think I would need from someone. I've laughed more than I have in a while since you came around." She paused, and he waited for her to speak. Grant was sure she was going to tell him that she could do better. He certainly had been thinking that for the last several hours. "I think I could get used to you hanging around. I was serious when I told you I don't do mushy shit. It's not who I am."

When she slipped into the restaurant ahead of him, Grant found himself tickled by what she'd just said to him. Because for as much as she said she wasn't the mushy type, he was. His mom had told him how to woo a woman and what to do with one that you liked. He was going to mushy her as much as he possibly could. It felt like she'd tossed down the gauntlet, and he was there to pick it up.

Dinner was nice. He wasn't surprised by the amount of food she could put away. Piper didn't comment on his appetite, either. They not only enjoyed the salad bar that was his favorite part of this place, but he also enjoyed the company. Piper was both comical as well as intelligent.

Just as he was ready to comment on how much fun he was having, he felt an unfamiliar touch to his mind.

*Hello, Grant. It's Duncan, in the event you don't know.* He said he didn't and was glad he could speak to him thusly. *Yes, well, you might not think that once the two of you return. As I said to you, my mother had plans for the two of you. I can tell you now, then have you tell Piper, which is what I'd prefer, so I don't get hurt. Or you can wait until you return and I'll tell you both at the same time.*

*Since I'm new to this relationship, I'm going to let you tell us.* Duncan told him he was a spoilsport. *Perhaps so. But I'm enjoying myself too much for it to be messed up because you're afraid of your birds.*

*Yes, I guess there is that. By the way, you two did a good job with the fire. The people have been brought to justice, and the owners of the place aren't going to be blamed for what happened. All good as far as I can see. With the exception of the deaths of all those people. That hurts me more than I think I could explain to you.* Grant told him it hurt him as well. *I would imagine. With your connection to the earth, you would have felt it worse than even I. Thank you for your help, Grant. I know it hurt both of you to be involved, but so much more has been accomplished with the two of you working together.*

*I started to say it was my pleasure. And in a way, I guess it was. But it was nice to be able to use my magic to help out the humans.* Duncan asked him when they'd be back. *I don't know. This is Piper's job, not mine. I only came along to be with her. I can ask her, but I think she's just too exhausted now to make that sort of decision.*

*I can understand that, as well. I'll look forward to talking to you both when you return. You will shield me, as your king, if I piss her off too much, won't you?* Duncan was laughing, so Grant didn't see any reason to tell him he was on his own against his mate. *I'll speak to you both later. Goodnight, Grant.*

He didn't have any idea what the man would want of him. Nor did he really care. He had a mate, and he was willing to bet she'd have no trouble whatsoever in telling him off. Paying the bill with the company card, Grant was glad that Piper decided to head back tonight. He'd let the king know in the morning that they were home.

~*~

Benson waited while the phone was ringing. There was a great deal going on right now, and he'd bet his last nickel that he was going to somehow be blamed for it all. Well, not all of it, but at least the parts that would have him in— "Hello? I was wondering if it were possible to speak to Mr. Dante? Could you tell him I won't take up much of his time? Just a moment or two, please." The man that had answered the phone told him he could take a message and see if he'd call him back. "Good. That would be good. Just let me think a moment. I do need to speak to him. It's...I'm not threatening you or anything, but it's about his son, Abraham. He's newly adopted him."

"May I ask your name, sir?" He told him his name was Benson Lawrence. "Would you mind hanging on for one moment, sir? Mrs. Dante is here now. She would like to speak to you."

He was put on hold, and Benson had to tell himself to be calm. He didn't want to scare the woman just because he knew Retha better than they did. When the woman answered the phone, he could hear the anger in her voice.

"My name is Benson Lawrence. I'm the biological father of Abraham. I'm not sure what his last name is right now. When Retha left my home several years ago, she was going by Bundy." The woman didn't say anything, and Benson took that as a good sign. "I'm not with her. This other man—I think her actual husband, Tag Bundy—is with her and coming toward your home. I'm not sure what her plans are for Abraham, but it can't be good. She and I...it was a one night stand as far as sex was concerned. Then about a year or so later—"

"Why are you calling here, Mr. Lawrence?" He told her that was what he was getting to. "Just cut to the chase.

You assured my staff that you're not going to cause any trouble. Yet you calling here has upset my household. Not to mention, upset me. I'm not one to fuck with."

"No, ma'am. I can understand that you're not. Retha will hurt Abraham if she gets him from you. She's done it before. She lived with me for a little while, a few months after the little boy was born. Then one day, I came home from work, and she was gone. I didn't let it go. I probably should have, but I found someone to look for her for me. When they caught up with her, she no longer had Abraham. I thought for sure that she'd murdered him. Then I read about that place in the paper and went there. That's where I figured out about you and your husband." She asked him what he meant by that. "I'm thinking you're not very trusting. But that's a good thing nowadays. I read about the thing with the children's home. They didn't have a list of names to go with it, but I did some of my own searching and found that Abraham and a girl by the name of Tracy were adopted. Well, that's not true. They were all adopted, but I was able to narrow it down to you and your husband. I'm just trying to keep him safe from her. She's not what one might call maternal."

"What is it you want out of this, Mr. Lawrence? I'm not going to turn Abe over to you. If that's what you're thinking, then you'd better change your mind. As I told you before, I'm not one to fuck with." He said he wasn't in a position to raise anyone right now. "And the reason you say that? You're not going to come here either if you're planning something with Retha. We know she's on her way here. We assumed that Abe's biological father was with her."

"No. I.... When Abe came to live with me for a while, I did one of those DNA tests. I only had a one night thing with Retha. To be honest, Mrs. Dante, I don't even remember much of it. I've never been one to indulge in liquor or the like. But that next morning, I woke with a splitting headache, my money gone, and no memory of much of anything. Retha was there. She acted like we had this long term thing going on, and I kicked her to the curb. Then about a year later, she comes around with this kid." Benson sat down on his couch. "I don't want anything from you. I swear. It's a bit too late for me, anyway. She gave me AIDS, you see, and I'm not long for this world. She's the only person that...Retha is the only person I've ever slept with. And I don't think she even knows she's sick yet."

"I'm so sorry, Mr. Lawrence. I truly am." He felt his eyes fill up. More tears wouldn't help him out, he told her, but he did want to make sure the one thing he could be proud of was safe. "I'm sending someone for you. I want you to come here to our home and see what you can help us with concerning Retha."

"No, ma'am, that's all right. Like I said, I wanted to make sure that Abraham is safe, that's all." She told him that someone by the name of Grant was going to be there within the next hour. "You don't know anything about me, miss. What if I'm some sort of scammer?"

"If you are, when you arrive, you won't have to worry about dying that horrific death. I'll make sure you suffer much worse." He believed her too. Telling her he'd be there, he asked if she needed his address. "No. I have it. As well as your medical records. You'll see that we're not a family that anyone messes with. Retha won't know what hit her. You'll come here, we'll work things out, and then we'll talk. Be ready."

After the line went dead, Benson laid back on the couch. He wasn't feeling up for much of anything today. Not just feeling sick, but the doctor hadn't given him a good prognosis. He had less than two months left.

Benson had always thought of himself as a good person. He'd been the type of man that would get up from his seat to give it to someone else. If he had more than enough, which had been often enough, he'd share it with those that lived around him. He had friends, money in the bank, as well as a good outlook on life. Then Retha.

The DNA test hadn't come back until she left him again. The boy was ninety-nine percent his. That, he thought, was about as close as it could get. While the two of them had been living with him, Benson knew that Abraham was much smarter than the average kid. By the time he was three months old, he'd been showing signs of being extremely intelligent. Retha hated when Benson pointed that out to her, so he stopped. That didn't keep him from encouraging the little boy. Then he was gone.

A friend of his, a cop, had told him that the police had been trying to stop the selling of children on the black market. Every day he'd ask Mac if his son had come through. Then one day, he told him he'd been there. But before either of them could retrieve him from the hospital, he was gone again. Stolen, they said. That was when Benson lost all hope of finding him again. Until he read about the children's home. But again, he was too late to find his son.

Someone at the door woke him from his nap. Benson staggered to the door, his body getting weaker every day, and opened it. His timing could have been better, he supposed. He opened it in time to hear Mrs. Sheradon from across the hall telling the man at the door that Benson had that nasty disease. That the man should go home to his wife.

"I'm his wife, you old goat. Get your skinny ass back in that room before I have to make an example of you. Get." Mrs. Sheradon closed her door with a snap, and the beautiful woman that had threatened her smiled at him. "Hello, Mr. Lawrence. My name is Piper Coby. This man is my husband, Grant. You were told to expect us?"

"Yes. I'm sorry. I just woke up." The man picked him up when Benson started for the couch again. "I'm sorry. The doctor told me I don't have long to live. Please, make sure you clean up well. I'd hate to have you get what I have."

The man, Grant, looked at his wife. When she nodded, the most extraordinary thing happened. The man put his hand over his chest, and Benson felt...well, he felt wonderful. Like every bit of his body was given a power-up like they give you in games.

"You'll have to rest for a little while. In the meantime, I'm going to order us some food." Grant told Piper he'd go get something. When he kissed the woman goodbye, Benson had a feeling he'd startled her with the kiss. Shaking his head, he wondered what was going on. Piper sat across from him. "All right. In the event you have no idea what just happened, I'll explain. Grant cured you of everything you had recently. You'll live a full and good life. If, and this is a huge if, you don't fuck up. If you do, I will shift into my bird and burn you to a fucking crisp. I'm a phoenix, and I'm well within my rights to murder you where you sit."

He stared at her for several seconds before he nodded. Under normal circumstances, he would have laughed at her, or at the very least, called her a liar. But he was feeling good, better than he had in years, and he knew it was because of something unspoken between her and Grant. She leaned back on the chair she was sitting on.

"You believe me." He said he had no reason not to believe her. He, as a matter of fact, was feeling too good to doubt her. "Abe has no idea that we're here to get you. We've not told him anything about you saying you're his biological father either. And until we can figure out what kind of scam you're running—if any, I mean—then he won't. He's a wonderful kid, and there isn't any way I'm going to see him hurt again."

"Did Retha hurt him?" Nothing. Not even a blink of her eye. "I have a feeling he was one of the children that were raped in that home, wasn't he? You don't have to answer me. But I do want you to know that had I known he was there, I would have gone to get him. I tried to buy him when Retha put him up for sale a few years ago. But somehow, she slipped by me, and the police and I missed him."

"Jude said you had a DNA test done. Why didn't you take that to the police when you found out he was your son?" He told her about how he was dying. "You're not now. You won't—unless, as I said, you fuck up. How long did she live with you? Retha. Did she hurt Abe when he was here?"

"She lived here with him for a few months. About three, I think. Abe was about three months old when she arrived. As for her hurting him? I'm not sure if you consider neglecting him hurting him, but I do. Retha ignored him over partying the entire time she was here. I didn't say anything to her. I wanted to make sure Abe was well taken care of. Then about six weeks after she up and left, I found out that I have AIDS. I'd not slept with her when she returned. I got it from her when she conceived Abe." Again, he felt the tears fill his eyes. "If you end up ending my life, could I please, just once, see him? From a distance, if that's all I can have. I've been worried about him since he was brought here."

She went to the door and opened it just as Grant was there. When he came in, he put the large bag on the table and went to help Benson up. He wasn't nearly as weak as he had been, but he was still unsteady on his feet. Glad for the help and the food, he bawled like a baby when they sat the boxes of Chinese food in front of him.

"Come on, big guy. Eat up, and we'll be on our way." Grant spoke to him in a soft voice. There was no censure to what he was saying, either. While the two of them spoke about speaking to Duncan about something, he gathered himself up and fixed his plate. He'd not had a good hot meal in a long time. Eating slowly so as not to be sick, Benson was able to join in the conversation with them when he could. When they were ready to leave, Piper told him he'd be just fine while Grant helped him to the large limo outside of his place.

Money. They had it, he realized. More than just a little too, he'd bet. Benson only hoped he'd get to make sure Abe was all right. Just once. Closing his eyes, he rested until they got to the airport. Then he slept in the bed on the private plane they'd come to get him in. His last thought before he fell into a deep sleep was that he hoped they didn't drop him from the plane. With a smile, he slept.

When Grant woke him, it took him a second or two to remember where he was. The smile on the man's face made Benson realize two things. He wasn't human, and he was genuinely a nice guy. After he sat up, Grant told him he should be better now, and Benson said he was feeling very well.

"Good. We've been talking to Jude and Duncan, Abe's parents. They said if you do something stupid—"

"Yes, they'll kill me." He smiled when Grant did. "They're a very violent group, aren't they? When I was speaking with Jude earlier, she was very determined to make sure I understood what was going to happen. Not that I blame them. But I promise I will try not to piss them off. This is an opportunity I never thought I'd get."

"See that you don't. We're headed to the castle when you're ready."

He nodded and started to ask Grant if it really was a castle, but he was gone again. Benson thought a castle was just what they called their home. Wherever they lived or whatever sort of house they had, Benson was going to be on his best behavior while there.

# Chapter 4

Retha wasn't sure what the fuck was going on, but now she couldn't find the house she'd been told her son was at. They said it was on Castle Street or something like that. But all she'd been able to find with that street address was a couple of showplaces that looked like castles, as well as a whole lot of hillbillies running around like fools.

"I've never seen so many people working out in their yards before. Have you?" She told Tag that she saw someone working in a garden too. "Why? Don't they have enough grocery stores around here? Whatever they're growing, it can't be all that good for them. Look how much time it took for that lady out there to dig up potatoes. I didn't even know potatoes grew in the ground, did you?"

"I never really thought about it." Retha looked

around. They were sitting at a big picnic table, having an ice cream cone. "Who the hell would have thought there'd be places around that still served up ice cream? I've not seen one of them kinda shops since I was a kid."

The cone was delicious. When Retha was asked if she wanted a waffle cone or a homemade one, she opted for the homemade. It was the most wonderful thing she'd ever eaten. The inside of it was coated with the richest chocolate she'd ever tasted. The ice cream was so good she wanted a big bowl of it to eat by herself. But there wasn't enough money for that.

Her plan had been to take the homemade one and send it back for being nasty. But once she saw the girl working the backline whip one up for her, she decided to give it a try. Boy, oh boy, she was never sending this sucker back.

"I've been watching the people here. They're sure a friendly bunch. Did you hear that guy ask that woman if she wanted to join him and his family for dinner tonight? I can't even remember the last time we were invited to have food with someone. Must be something else to have friends like that." She told him they had friends. "We do. But not a one of them invites us over for dinner."

"No. I'm sure everyone we know is struggling too. Just wait until we get the boy back. Then we'll be on easy street. Did I tell you I contacted that man about selling him off? He said he didn't do stuff like that anymore. I wonder what got up his ass." Tag told her he'd heard the police were cracking down on stuff like that more and more. "Yeah, I suppose so. You know why, don't you? They want to make it so no one can make any money but themselves. I'd bet anything that there are cops all over the place that are stealing kids away to sell."

She didn't have any idea if that was going on or not. Retha enjoyed saying things like that. It made her feel like she was a good deal smarter than she really was. The thing was, Retha couldn't spell much of anything. Nor could she read. Signing her name was the best she could do, but only if she had time to think about each letter. While she knew her name, it was hard for her to remember in what order the letters went.

They were just talking about how to get another cone when a woman sat down with them. She didn't even ask if she could but plopped her ass down like she owned the place. When she told her she did indeed own the place, Retha told her to go away.

"I think I need to stick around and tell you two some things you're not aware of." Tag asked her like what. "Well, for one thing, you're not going to get Abe. He's not going to go anywhere near you. Also, and you might find this hard to believe since we've only just met, but I don't like you."

"Well, is that so? You just wait a minute, and I'll think on how much I don't care what you like or don't. How do you know we're here for the kid?" She told him his name. "I know what it is, you cunt. Where is he?"

"Home with his sister and parents. Don't call me a cunt again. Also, if I were you, I'd care a great deal about what makes me like or dislike you. It could be the only thing in the world that saves you. Not that I think you'll just go away. But Abe, he told us he wanted you both dead." That did surprise her. She hadn't remembered his name until just then. "He's happy. Going to college and having a wonderful life. Until he realized, I guess, that you two are going to try and mess things up for him."

"He messed up a lot of shit for me too. You tell him that." She realized that the woman knew where he was. "I want to talk to him. Now. I want him to tell me why he wants me dead."

"I can tell you that. You sold him off, for starters. You and this man have been abusing him since he was born. Why didn't you just leave him with Benson? He would have been a lot better off if you had. Of course, my sister and her husband wouldn't have been able to adopt him if that had happened." An ice cream cone appeared in the woman's hand, and it took Retha a few seconds to take her eyes off the treat. "I'd give you this, but I haven't had time to put any poison in it yet. Next time. I promise."

"You said he was in college. That ain't right. He's not even five yet. You're a liar." The woman, she'd never said her name yet, just looked at Tag. "If you think we're going to believe a thing that comes out of your mouth, you're stupider than that kid is."

"Abe is about to turn ten. Good job there in keeping

up with the times. By the way, you should know two more things. I'm not human. I'm a bird of prey. Mercy is my name, but I've come to realize I don't have a great deal of that when dealing with morons like the two of you. The second thing is that I'm going to kill you. Not easily, either." Retha scrambled back from Mercy when her hair and arms started to sprout feathers. Big fucking ones too. "I had it in my head that I was going to snap the two of you in half then eat you down, but I think the two of you are poisonous enough to perhaps make me sick for a while. So that is out. Also, I thought about taking you out to sea. Just leaving you there. I know that neither of you can swim. We're out there looking for something anyway as of this morning, and it might be entertaining to watch the two of you sink to the bottom of the waterway."

"You're insane. You can't just tell somebody that and think it's going to be all right with them." Mercy asked Tag if he thought anyone would care. "I will. Damn it all to fuck and back. You can't say that sort of thing. What if I believed you?"

"You should." If she'd not been looking right at Tag, she wouldn't have believed it. Not only did he rise up from the seat he'd been sitting on, but he turned blue. "Right now, I can snap your neck, and not one person here would care one bit. Even if I were to change into my bird and pick you up by my claws, no one would come to your aid. No one wants you around."

"You're killing him." Retha looked around. There were people having cones, but not one of them came to ask what Mercy was doing. "Let him go, damn it. That's my husband you're killing."

Just as she thought Mercy was really going to kill him, he flew across the parking lot and hit the brick building there. Retha knew he was dead. The way he was bleeding down the wall and with his head all smashed made her think the woman was stronger than she looked.

Mercy looked at her. Anger. It was as strong on her face as anything Retha had ever seen before. Backing away from her, she stopped moving when she was lifted up as well. Closing her eyes, Retha just knew she was going to be joining her husband as a freaky art project on the wall behind her.

"I should end you right now for what you've done." Clawing at her throat, she couldn't even ask her what she was talking about. "You passed those little boys around like they were chips in a fucking bowl. Where are they? Where are Abe's brothers now?"

"Dead." Retha had forgotten about her other sons. They'd been dead for so long that they weren't even a slight memory anymore. As the woman stood up, a woman appeared behind her. She looked as confused as Mercy did angry.

"Mercy? What's going on?" The woman behind Mercy spoke, but Mercy didn't answer her, or at least not so that Retha could hear. However, she couldn't see anything in front of her anymore. Black and blue spots had appeared before her eyes. "Kill her. Christ, kill her before Jude and Duncan find out what she's done."

Retha felt herself flying through the air. Just as she hit the wall where Tag had been killed, Retha knew she'd be lucky to die this way. The way that the two women had looked at her, she thought for sure they'd make her death longer.

~*~

Piper had taken care that the stain on the wall was gone. Not only did she clean up, but she took the memory of what had happened from the people there. She knew she'd never forget what Mercy had shown her. The images of those poor children would haunt her for the rest of her days, she thought.

"May I join you?" After she nodded at Grant, he sat down on the chair across from her. "I've spoken to Duncan. He said in light of what happened today, he's all right with scheduling the meeting with us tomorrow. Are you all right with that?"

"I am. Would you go out to the dive with me? I really would enjoy that, I think. Mercy told me they've found a great many artifacts already. As well as several trunks that none of us knew were on the ship. Joel said you were a great help. We had no idea you could dive so deeply." He told her it was the fae in him. "I suppose. They're very strong creatures. Did they help you breathe under the water as well?"

"Yes. Do you not want to talk about what happened today?" She shook her head. "All right. Yes. I can dive for longer periods when necessary. Joel is suited up in that thing Mercy found for him. I think she'd only have to give him a little magic, and he'd not need it. However, knowing Joel, he'd want things to be just perfect for him to want to go underwater. Or anything for that matter. I'm enjoying looking at the things they thought would be necessary to bring to a new place. I would guess you'd need a lot when traveling so far. But the jewelry I was able to bring up is something else."

"Jude and Duncan are going to divide up the things they brought up between the six of us first. She said that way we can use it for some project we can fund with it. She had four children by Tag. They sold them to others to have sex with." He said he knew and was sorry. "Do you know what is going to happen to the other things that are brought up? I mean, from what I remember, there were bodies on the ship as well. I doubt they'd be there anymore. Not after all this time."

"There were a few bones lying around. I found a few, but nothing much more than that. There were chain leggings in the bottommost part of the ship. Mercy said that was where the woman was." Piper said she remembered that now. "Dante made sure that her family, what was left of them, was well compensated for their loss before she died. I never realized she could see into the future. The king, he killed the woman's entire family to have her simply because she had sons and no daughters."

"Dante figured he was going to come here, demand that she marry him, then kill her on their wedding night. The other woman, the one on the ship, was going to be his wife when Dante was dead. No one, it seemed, cared a bit for him dying. There was never a missive sent here to find out where he was." Grant told her there had been an inquiry about his death, but nothing more than that. "They would have seen the castle and figured that a storm had knocked the boat off voyage and it was lost at sea. I have to tell Abe what Mercy and I have done."

"He knows." She looked at Grant. "Jude told him what the two of you had seen. Not a lot of details, only that you saw that he'd had siblings, and they were killed as a result of their parents' actions. I think he might have an idea of what happened, but he didn't say anything. Jude told us he was sleeping when she left him. Abe hugged her after she told him. He has not been sleeping well since he found out how close they were. I love you, Piper."

"I've fallen in love with you as well. I wasn't sure at first, I will tell you that. You were there for me a great deal, holding my hand or even just being near to me when I needed it. It occurred to me while sitting out here that you've never asked me for anything. Not that you would—everything I have is yours anyway. But right now, you could ask me for the world, and I'd make sure you got it." She looked away before continuing. "I've decided I'm going to find a way to make sure sexually abused children have someplace to go. I don't have a great many details right now, but I'll work them out with you. If you'll help me."

"Yes. I would very much like to help you with that." She nodded. "There are ways that we can keep kids safe, too, I think. As we're both fae, we can have the earth tell us when a child is being hurt badly. I'm sure it happens a great deal more than we'd be able to take care of all the time, but with our magic, we can scoop them up and bring them someplace safe."

"I love that idea. I know there are times when a child thinks they're being abused when they're only being taught right from wrong. That's not abuse, but parenting. Somewhere along the line of having children, I believe we've forgotten that part of being an adult." He told her he agreed with her one hundred percent. "Did you know that I can't see into Jude's mind? I never could read any of them, but it's different now. I used to even be able to see things in Jude's mind that weren't blocked. Like something that was making her upset or happy. I can't see a thing in her head, nor Duncan's. It's like a thick wall has been put up, and I can't breach it."

"What is it you were looking for?" She told him. "Ah. Yes, I can understand how you'd want to know how they felt about you and Mercy killing the other two. However, I don't think they care. From the beginning,

I think they knew they'd end up dead. I think the way they were killed was much easier on them than either Jude or Duncan would have done to them."

"I think you're right." She stood up, and Grant did as well. "I'd like to talk to Duncan now. If he's available. Then I want to lock us in our bedroom and get to know each other in the best possible way."

"I love the way your mind works."

They were walking hand in hand as they made their way into the house. Piper could get used to depending on someone else for some of her happiness. She, for sure, could be happy just living in their own home and doing what other couples did, whatever that might be. Smiling to herself, Piper wanted the mushy stuff too, she just realized.

~*~

"No. I mean, just no." Grant looked over at Piper when she spoke to Duncan. Grant had been trying his best not to laugh since Duncan made his big announcement. "You need Mercy to do that. Mercy is the oldest, and she and Joel should go there. Not me. I mean, it's not my place."

"I believe we both understand that Mercy is not the type of person to help others get their lives back on track. The castle has been updated magically, and it has all the comforts of home. All you need to do is—"

"I don't think you're hearing me. I said no. I don't want to run a castle with Grant. No offense to him, but

I don't have time to wetnurse a bunch of people that should have figured out their lives before now." Duncan stood up, and so did Grant. "Don't worry about him. He's not going to hurt me. I'm stronger than he is."

"Perhaps you were at one time." When Piper began pacing the room, Duncan looked at him. "There are seventy people living on the outside of the keep. The walls were sealed up right after my mom realized that Burt, the lord of that castle, was dead, along with her own husband. When I say sealed up, I mean she removed any windows and doors to the place, and the drawbridge to get into the keep was turned to stone. No one has been in it for hundreds of years."

"It must be a mess then. Why would you even consider sending us there to take care of things? For that matter, why are you sending us away anyway? Is it because of us killing that couple? I'd do it again if I had to. They were monsters." Duncan told Piper it had nothing to do with that. His mom had said it. "Your mom said to send us away?"

Grant could hear the pain in her voice. She was feeling discarded. Unworthy. He could feel it like it was his own pain. When she sat down beside him, Grant took her hand. She was in so much pain he wasn't sure she'd listen to Duncan at all now.

"They aren't sending you away. Will you get your head out of your ass for one second, Piper? Christ. Listen to what he's telling you." Mercy grabbed Piper by the shoulders and turned her to face her while they both sat on the couch. "He's sending the best there, and that would be the two of you. Can you imagine me going there and having someone whine at me that they don't have enough to eat? I'd tell them to go hunting or some other shit like that. Of course, you'd tell them that too, but you'd be much nicer about it. We both know I'm not nice to humans. They're stupid and can't seem to think and walk at the same time."

"I'm human." Joel laughed. "Or I was at one time." Mercy just had to look at him. "Okay, I get it. I wasn't very smart when we first met. Go on. Ignore the one time human in the corner."

"How will we have dinners together? I won't have any of you around to just hang out with." Duncan pointed out that it was only a two hour drive from their keep to this one. Less if she flew. "I don't have any idea why she'd pick me. I can't be depended on to take care of people. My studio is a testament to my inability to keep things straight."

Grant laughed. He could no more have held it in than he could have told Piper no about anything she wanted from him. When she turned and glared at him, he kissed her on the mouth, then kissed her again. There was something so cute about Piper when she was pissy.

"I, for one, would like to help out with the castle and the occupants that have settled there. I'm assuming these people have no rights to where they're living?" Duncan told him they were, for the most part, squatters. "So do you want them removed, or do you want them to figure out how to live there legally?"

"That would be something you two would figure out. I'm all for them staying, if they follow any rules, you would impose on them. They would have to have homes built. For the most part, they're living in campers and tents. A few have been clever enough to have some kind of semi-permanent home. But that is something else you'd have to take care of. There is plenty of money for you two to make any kind of improvements to the housing they're living in. Also, my mom made sure there are trees and a garden there for the keep to use. From what I've read in the journals she kept, as soon as Piper crosses over the threshold, everything will come alive and start producing."

"You said it was all locked up. I don't understand how that is supposed to work with me crossing over the threshold." She glared at Grant. "Not that we're going to do it, right? You want to live by your mom, don't you?"

"I don't want to upset you anymore than you are, love, but we'd already planned on my mom staying with us. Did you know she was the sometimes cook in this castle? I bet she would have all kinds of advice for us running the other one." Grant asked Duncan how large the castle was. "I mean, you said it was updated. Do we have lights and heat? Or do we even have running water?"

"Whatever is in this castle is in the other one. According to the journal again, Mom said the improvements would be duplicated in both of them at the same time. So you'd not just have heat and lights, but Internet and cable as well. And of course, running water." Duncan handed him a file. "I'm not sure how much that is going to help you, but it was within the paperwork that was here. As you can see, that castle is larger than this one because it had been added onto at some point. I think it had something to do with brother rivalry. Anyway, there is a smokehouse on the grounds, as well as an herb drier. I'm not entirely sure what that might be, but you have it and a large herbal garden. My aunt, my uncle's wife, was said to have had the best herbs around back then. Again, I'm not sure what that will mean for the two of you."

"These people that we're supposed to be taking care of. Are there jobs for them to do? I mean, are they just sponging off the land and will expect the two of us to take care of them? Look, I don't want to have to go in there and replant the lot of them. If they've been lazing about for decades only to have them invite their friends around to do the same thing, I'm going to be sorely pissed off." Duncan handed her some photos, and Grant looked them over as well. "They're not even cleaning up after themselves? Oh no, they're not going to be doing this when I get there. We're going to have order and a place to dump trash. Not leave it— Is that a stroller there? Someone is actually raising a child in this sort of environment? That's it, I'm going there today and taking care of this shit."

"So, you're going to take it?" Duncan looked at Grant when all Piper did was fold her arms over her chest and tap her foot at him. "I don't know what that means. Is she all right with it now?"

"I would say she is. However, if I've learned anything in my years on this planet, it's that you never assume anything when it comes to having a mate. Or any female." Grant pulled Piper into his arms and felt her relax against him. "We're in love. I just wanted to put that out there. Also, I will do what she wants. If that means staying in the tiny house myself and my mom have lived in together, then that's good too. However, if my opinion matters, I think that even without me, Piper could make this work on a great many levels that I'm betting not even you have thought of."

Piper looked up at him, then at Jude and Duncan. Duncan had been doing all the talking, and Jude just sat there. Grant thought that was totally out of character for her but waited. When she had something to say, Grant was sure it would not only be profound but also just what Piper needed to hear to make her know she could do this for them.

"There are nine children out in those houses. I've not spoken to them, nor the adults. But I can tell you this. Their living conditions are horrific. You'll do this for me, won't you, Piper? I need to know those kids are safe from harm. I don't know how they were able to survive this long with how they're living. But they need you to get up off your ass and help them." Jude hugged Piper and him together. "They need a strong hand and a gentle word. I think we both know you can do both. And if not, let Grant here be the gentle word."

They were all laughing when they sat down to lunch. After this, they were going to go back out to the site and see about what else was brought up. Whatever it was, Grant was going to ask Duncan if he could buy the ruby ring he'd found when he'd been diving for them.

He loved rubies. However, this one had been in a nice box and hadn't been harmed at all from being in the deep for so long. When he'd opened the box, pulling out the ring, he gasped with the beauty. Holding it up to the sunlight, the colors reflected on the boat decking were so like Piper's hair that he could only see this ring on her finger. Even Mercy, who had been out on the boat with him at the time, commented on how much it was like her hair.

"I heard someone say to her once that it looked as if she'd dipped her hair into a setting sun to make it look as it does. I think that is the very reason everyone believes her when she tells them she's a phoenix. There is no doubting she has the colors all right." Grant asked her if she liked rubies. "Yes. She used to make jewelry at one time, a long time ago. She would find rubies, believe it or not, and use them in all sorts of things like that. Then one day, she decided she wanted to use them in a phoenix. If you get to see the one she made in her studio, look at her. The bird is covered in gems of all sorts and colors. To me, it's one of the most beautiful pieces she'd ever created."

"It's still wrapped up in the barn behind the castle."

At that time, they were both looking for a place to live. Now that they'd be moving to the other castle, he wondered what she'd do with it. Hopefully, she'd display it where everyone that came to see them would see that his mate was a very talented artist.

By the time they were ready to see what other treasures they could find, the crew that was doing most of the lifting was ready to go back out as well. The things they'd discovered were being stored away in the lower levels of the castle. He couldn't wait to get it all finished so they could have fun opening the sacks and other containers that had been pulled up.

"Before I forget, there is a trunk for you." He asked Piper what sort of trunk. "I'm not sure what might be in yours, but mine had all sorts of things that sparked memories from when I lived around here. I guess we can assume since she knew you were going to be my mate, that there are things there for you to have memories of as well. Also, in my trunk, there were crowns. Until now, I had no idea why she'd leave them for me. I'm assuming they're from the castle we're going to."

"Is this something you really want to do, Piper? I know we've sort of bullied you into it." She said she was warming up to the idea. "Good. I think it'll be fun for you and I to have something we can call our own like this. We'll run it well, I believe. I'm just hoping we don't have too much trouble with the squatters. I'd hate to have to call in the police to have them moved on. I wonder just how long they've been living there."

"Less than five years, Duncan told me." He said that wasn't terribly long. "No. But it might be for them. I just can't believe anyone would subject their children to such conditions—no running water, no heat. I know for a fact that the weather up here can change in a heartbeat. That's the first thing we're going to tackle. Either getting them off the property or fixing it, so they have adequate housing."

He didn't point out to her that she'd not answered the question as to whether or not she wanted to do this. However, he had a feeling that someone was currently packing up their things for the move. Grant wondered if he could get himself a truck, just because it would be nice to haul things back and forth from the store. Also, a tractor. Thinking that he needed to slow it down a bit, had him laughing. They didn't even know when they were moving in, much less if they'd be welcomed by the people.

The water was warm, he'd discovered earlier. Diving off the side of the boat and into the water was as much fun as he'd had in a while. When Piper dove in with him, they went to the bottom of the waterway together. He was ready to not just discover things here, but with her. Grant was as excited as he'd ever been in starting a new chapter of his life.

# *Chapter 5*

Benson was afraid to feel this good. There had to be a catch. Lying in the big bed he'd been in for the last couple of days, he also couldn't believe how well he'd been sleeping. All through the night without having to get up once to take a pain pill hadn't happened to him in five years. Rolling to his side, thinking about getting up, he saw a young boy sitting in the chair next to the bed. It looked like he was reading *War and Peace*.

"Is it any good?" The child put the book down on his lap and told him it was really good but was also colorful. "In what way colorful?"

"The author describes each thing very well. Like if you could just close your eyes while reading it, you'd be able to see it. I like books like that. This book is good, but I enjoy science fiction better. I'm Abe, your biological son." Benson sat up but didn't say anything. "I talked to my mom and dad about you yesterday. They said that I could come up here and talk to you. If you didn't mind."

"No. I don't mind. How much do you know about me?" Abe told him only what they could find out. "I suppose that's not really a lot, is it?"

"Mom told me that you had AIDS. That you were dying. I'm glad they were able to heal you and bring you here. I've been wanting to talk to you anyway." Benson nodded. "I've been thinking about what to call you. I know you're my biological dad. I understand too that you and my biological mom had sex one time and that she murdered you with her poisoned body. If it's all right with you, because we don't know each other at all, I'd like to call you Uncle Benson. If that bothers you, we can think of something else."

"I don't have an issue with you calling me your uncle. I think that's about the easiest way for the two of us to go forward. I don't know how long I'll be around, however. I'm not quite sure why they bothered with me at all." Abe explained what he knew. "I'm immortal? I don't suppose you know what that means. I understand the word, but not what terms there are with it."

"You'll not die or be sick anymore. Also, you won't age. I will up until I'm about twenty-five, then after that, I'll not look any different. The living forever stuff is complicated, and I don't understand a lot about it. I guess I could look it up, but I doubt there will be much, as no one will believe that someone can live forever. Anyway.

I'd like for you to stay here. I'd like to get to know you. But I have parents now, and I love them very much. So the uncle thing will have to be forever too." Benson told him that he was fine with that as well. "Good. Mr. Bloom—he was a good friend of mine—he gave me his house when he passed away. I loved him too, and if he'd been around longer, I might have gotten to adopt him as my grandda. But he left me his house, as I said. I want you to live there until you can find a better place. Or not. You can stay there for as long as you wish. The house is in good repair. Dad told me it would be better to have someone staying in it rather than letting it sit and rot away. I don't think Mr. Bloom meant for me to do that anyway."

"You have a house?" Abe smiled and nodded. "I don't have anything. Not even a home anymore. Once I got sicker, I lost a lot of things."

"This will be a good start for you then. Mom said, sometimes, it's good to have a clean slate. Sometimes you can remake yourself into whatever you want. I'd want to be just me, but she told me I was too young to make that sort of decision." Abe got up. "Come on downstairs, and we'll eat together. Then I'll see if Dad can take us to the house. You can stay here for as long as you want. Mom said the house would need to be aired out and cleaned up. It'll be nice for you to be there. I can ride my bike to see you whenever I want. Won't that be fun?"

Benson entered the kitchen and found the rest of the family there. He didn't say much to them. He wasn't even sure what he could say to them. They'd saved him, opened their home for him, and all he'd done was sleep. Asking for something to eat, he wanted to beg them to let what Abe had been telling him to be true.

"It is." He looked at who he thought was Jude. He didn't remember names well from a few days ago. "Come on, Benson, join us for lunch. You were right. I'm Jude. This is my husband, Duncan. Everything Abe has told you is true. We'd love for you to stay and get to know him. Also, as he said, the house is there for you to use. It's a lovely older house. Furnished and well maintained. It just needs someone there to make it a home again."

"You don't know me. Why would any of you do this for a man down on his luck?" She asked him if it was true that he had been a physician. "Yes. I was a pediatric physician for a long time. But when it was discovered that I had AIDS, everyone dropped me, including the partnership I'd started. I can no longer afford my insurance either. So I guess I'm sort of a doctor."

"I think we can take care of all of that, including a nice salary for you." She asked him to sit down again. "My sister, Piper, and her husband are going to try and save as many abused children as they can. And when I say to save them, if necessary they're going to snatch them from the hands of the people hurting them, then that's the route they're going to go. We all agree it's far better to have them missing with us than to be missing and dead."

"You wish for me to help you by making sure they're healthy. I'd gladly do that for what you've done for me. But I don't think you having to pay me much is necessary. I have a home now. Food and friendships. Plus, I get to be uncle to this little guy." They all laughed, but Jude told him it was a done deal for him to make money. "We'll work something out on that if that's all right with you."

She didn't answer him but did smile. Benson thought he was going to be making what they said he would and that he'd just have to live with it.

As soon as the food was placed in from of him, he realized he was starving. Pacing himself so he'd not make himself sick, he ate smaller bites as he talked to the family. When Piper and Grant joined them, they told him more about what the job would involve.

"I like that. Having a cook in the home will make sure that I have plenty of time to take care of the little ones. And from what I've been told about the house, it's large enough for us to be able to take on as many children as you save." Piper told him she'd be getting some more beds in the rooms, with Abe's permission, to house children in rooms together. "That would be nice for some of the younger ones. Children that are terrified of being left alone, or worse, afraid of the dark, or just need someone there to hear their breathing. That's a nice thing to do for them. I've heard of children that were left on their own when the parent or someone watching over them had OD'd, and they were left with the bodies. Yes,

I can see where having others would be a good thing."

They spoke for another hour or so. Then they went to the Bloom house to look around. Benson couldn't believe he was going to be living here and doing something he loved so much—taking care of children. He was also going to see Abe grow up. Not that he wanted to be his father—he thought Duncan was doing a better job of that than even Benson's own parents had, and he had always thought they were great parents. No, Abe was in the perfect spot now, and he'd not do anything to mess that up for him.

The house was much nicer than he thought it might have been. Even from the outside, he thought the house was big. Going inside only made it seem like he was getting the better end of any deal they were making with him. Benson even thought the furniture was something he might well have picked out for his own home. He was sitting in one of the oversized chairs, enjoying the view out back when Molly, Grant's mom, joined him.

"I've heard a great deal about you from Piper and Grant. They said they were going to talk to you about having the children they rescue come here to be put back together. They didn't say that, but it's my understanding that you'll be doing a lot of medical work with them. Is that right?" He told her he hoped so. "I'd like to help you here. Move in with you and work from here. My son, he's going to take the other castle that belongs to Duncan, and I'd just be in the way. They said I wouldn't be, but I'm thinking that with them being newly together, I will be. I'm not saying we have to sleep together, but I'd love to live here because of the work you're doing, and you and I…. Well, I'm hoping we can get to know each other."

"I'd like that. I've heard a great deal about you as well. All of it glowing reports. Abe and his sister, they love you to pieces." Her face pinked up, and he smiled. "I'd be honored if you were to live here with me. I think, between the two of us, we'd be good for the children too."

"I thought so as well." She leaned back on the couch as if asking him to live here had exhausted her. "You have magic. Did they tell you that? Not as much as the others do, but you have some. Fae is a little of it. I'm not sure of the rest. I'm assuming Grant is the one that kept you from dying."

"He did. Do you know what I can do as a little fae?" She said that for the most part, he'd have to trial and error his magic. "I can understand that. Piper told me that sometimes magic mixes in a way that is different for each person. One thing I have discovered, quite by accident, is that I can change my clothes. I thought that to be the best. I've lost a great deal of weight of late, and I've not had much in the way of clothing that fits me."

"You more than likely have things that will make it easier to be around for a long time. Talents you didn't have before, such as cooking, and things you might have had a handle on, but nothing you were proficient at." He smiled at her. "I'm going to tell my son that you're all right with me staying here. I needed a place I could be in without my son. We've been together for such a long time that I'm fearful of missing him terribly. He's a good boy, my son, but he's got himself a mate now."

"Perhaps they'll have you grandchildren soon." She had such a hopeful look on her face that he hoped even if Piper and Grant didn't want children, they'd at least have one for this woman. "I've been wanting to ask but wasn't sure who it would be that I could ask without causing trouble. Are Retha and her husband still on their way here? I hate that they cause so much trouble for everyone."

"They're both dead." He didn't know if he wanted to ask what had happened, and Molly seemed to understand that. "They were in the area for about three hours, I guess, when Mercy and Piper came upon them. It was quick, much quicker than I think they deserved, but they're no longer a problem. I think, for the time being, we should just leave it at that."

"All right. Thank you for letting me know. Now I have enough information that I won't be making a fool of myself by asking." He thought about the two people and shivered. Whatever reasons the two women had to kill them, he was glad it was finished. Benson didn't know why, but he had a feeling it was about Abe, or something close to it. "I've been thinking about just keeping to one of the bedrooms down here. There are three of them.

Which would you like? I can move into another one if you wish the one I've picked. I took the one facing the side and back yards."

"How very nice of you. No, I'd like the one nearer the kitchen if you'd not mind. That will leave the one between us for you to use as an office should you need to." He said he'd not thought of that. "The family, they're going to outfit the basement with medical supplies for you. If you don't want every little gadget around, I'd try to get them a list."

"Yes. I've noticed they don't do things halfway. I think I'm going to enjoy living here with you. You're kind-hearted, and you don't seem to want much more than I do. A roof over our heads and a full belly." She said that was her in a nutshell and a garden in the summer. "Fresh things to eat sound wonderful. I've never had an opportunity to have even a plant where I was before. I think I'm also going to enjoy the outdoors if we're not too busy all the time."

The others joined them as he and Molly were out looking at the herb garden in the back. It was in need of a good weeding, as well as some of the things that would need to be transplanted. Piper said they had a lot of seeds they could plant that would help them. Benson was as excited as he'd ever been.

"I wanted to thank you for taking this on with us." He told Grant that it was his pleasure. "You might not think so if I have to wake you in the middle of the night too often. But we are going to make a difference here. And with your help, we might even be able to save a few children that would otherwise be dead. Thank you."

Benson shook hands with the older man. He knew, even though he looked like they were the same age, that Grant was thousands of years older than him. As they parted ways, he saw Molly ask to speak to Grant. He supposed they were going to talk about her moving in here to help. The two of them were old enough to make decisions on their own, he supposed, but he was happy she cleared it with her son before he found out on his own.

Benson went to find his room again. He was going to make that list before, as Molly said, he ended up with more equipment than he had room for.

~*~

The castle was much larger than Duncan's. Piper did wonder why Duncan and Jude had not moved into it instead of the other one, but she remembered that Duncan would want to be closer to his mom. She could understand that better than most. She missed Dante more the longer they were around here.

"How do you open it? I mean, is there a special word or phrase you use?" She told Grant she hadn't any idea but did touch her hand to the stoned off area where the drawbridge would be. "Do you feel the earth around us? I do. It's like everything is waiting for you to open up the magic the castle has. I'm not sure why that is how I feel, but it's there. A pause in their lives until we arrived."

"I can feel it here. The warmth of the stones. These stones would have been carved from the mountain behind it. Then brought here by the slaves that would have been doing most of the heavy work." She stood up and looked at where stone met stone against the mountain. Also, where the six turrets were. "I wonder why six? I mean, usually, a turret would have been built with a staircase in it, with windows. At least that is what I've discovered with Duncan's. Do you think we'll have six flights of stairs leading to the same part of the castle?"

"The middle ones are there for storage. It came in quite handy when we had stuff to sort and store. My name is Baker. I guess you could say I come with the house. The master of the house, he figured I was useful and spelled me to the stone here." Piper asked him what he was. "Troll. A runt too, but I'm a troll. My family kicked me to the side of the sea there and hoped I'd drown. The mistress of the castle, she found me, shook me out, and had me stay with her while the king of this place was away. He wasn't a good man, my lady. Cruelty was how he got what he wanted in everything."

"I've heard." He asked her if she was truly one of the birds. "I am—the phoenix. My mate here is fae. So you can see, we together have a good deal of magic. I'll free you from this place should you wish. I'd not have anyone here against their will, Baker."

"You'd do that too, wouldn't you?" She told him it

would be her pleasure to do that for him. "I should like to be freed so I can have a roam when I wish. I canna go no further than the walls of the keep now. But I'd be proud to work for you too."

"Thank you so much." She turned and looked at the castle. "I don't suppose you know how I'm supposed to cross over the threshold, do you? I could swim the waterway here, but I'd rather not. I don't know what's in that, but it needs to be cleaned up."

"You've only to drop a bit of your blood on the stone there." She asked him if he was sure. "Aye, I am, my lady. The mate too. Lord Grant will need to be welcome here as well, so that will be all it takes. But you'll need to move back. From what I've been told about the magic there, it works quickly."

She hadn't any idea what that might mean but cut open her palm and dropped a few drops of blood on the stone. When she was finished, Grant did the same. Backing away from the stones when the noises coming from the castle started, they all three stood there watching and waiting to see what would happen. Baker had been right. It did happen fast.

The large stone doorway laid down to rest on the stones they'd bled onto. It was a loud sound that hurt her ears more than she thought it might. As soon as she was across the stone drawbridge, she put her still bloodied hand on the wall of the castle, as did Grant. Grant pulled her away from it as soon as things started to move. And move they did.

The opening of the castle looked like the castle was just waking up from a long nap. The yawning hole there was larger than she'd ever seen on a castle, but it soon moved to be the same size as the stone they'd crossed to get in. Stepping back more, they all watched as not only did the windows open in the solid stone walls, but things inside the castle began to move around. From where they stood, they could see the walls stretching and moving. A stone table appeared in a room, along with a stone bench on either side. Then just as they appeared to be complete, they changed again into couches, as well as tables with lamps on them.

"Should we go in?" Baker said as soon as the castle was finished, they'd be able to enter. Not a moment before. "You mean if we tried to go in too early, the castle wouldn't allow it? That seems very magical. I'm assuming this is from the former queen?"

"It is. She might well have given it some magic I'm not privy to, but this, she told me, would make the home something you'd be able to raise children in. I'm not sure what that meant. Some of the people out yonder, they're raising them on a good deal less."

"Why don't we go and take care of the people while the castle finishes? Baker, if you'd like to come with us, I'd appreciate it. Just in the event they try and give us some trouble, you can be there as a witness to the facts." Baker told Grant he should expect trouble. "You know who these people are?"

"No, my lord. I could only see them from the turrets there. I could see them fighting among themselves and with the others. Nasty group of people if you were to ask me. The worst part is, they kill some of the creatures around here and leave what they don't want to rot. To me, that's a waste." They were headed toward the field that, if she remembered correctly from flying above it long ago, used to be filled with homes. Small cottages that had been for the people outside the keep. She asked Baker about it. "The homes, they were broken down by some people like these. Might well have happened to the castle had anyone been able to get into it. But they would come along, pick up the stones that made the houses and take them off. Or like these here, they'd just pile them up for their own uses. You be careful of them, my lady. They're a lot that has been getting things on their own for a while now."

They were in tents and makeshift houses. Tarps of every imaginable color on the roofs of some of the places were being held down by the same stones she was asking about. Most of them had outside fire pits, the smell coming off whatever they were cooking, making her gag a little. She ate worms as a bird, and that didn't smell nearly as bad as whatever was there. Instead of approaching them as herself, she shifted to her bird and landed on the shoulder of Grant. If he needed manpower, she thought as her bird, she'd be better help.

"Good. I nearly suggested that you come as your bird, but thought you'd want them to know who is in charge. I'm assuming this way, you're safer as well." She told him she was a good deal safer since she could still be ten times his size. "Good to know too. I'm thinking once they see you in that form, we'll not have any more trouble with them."

The first man they came upon came out with a gun in his hand. Piper didn't like that—the gun or the man. The two little children behind him looked as dirty as the water around the castle. They were skinny and smelled like they'd not had a bath in recent days. The man asked them what they wanted.

"You're trespassing. I know you were forewarned that someone was coming to live in the castle soon and that you had to be on your way. So this is me, as the owner of the castle and the lands around it, asking you once again to pack up and leave." The man just snorted. "Was that another language? I can tell you to leave in several if you were to tell me what one you speak."

"Huh?" The man looked as confused as anyone she'd ever seen before. Grant repeated his offer. "What the hell are you talking about? I'm speaking what I always speak."

"Oh. So you speak stupid. Okay. I think I can make that work too. You gotta leave right now." The man, if it was possible, looked more confused than before. "Leave here now, and I won't have to have you arrested."

"This here is my place." Grant told him it wasn't. "It is. See? I have my home here all set up. I even got family here that I'm taking care of."

"You don't seem to be doing such a good job of either if you ask me." The man said he'd not. "No, so you didn't. All right, Mr. Curtain. I'm going to give you an hour to be packed up and on your way. If not, I'm going to move you along faster by having you burnt out. It's up to you."

Grant moved through the next few people on the land. He met with the same lack of hospitality, the same claims, as well as people meeting him outside of whatever they were living in with a gun pointed at him. Piper thought warning them that they had to move had each of them gathering up a weapon of some sort and having their reasons all lined up for why they weren't leaving. Like they'd been given a script to read over.

They were headed back to Mr. Curtain after they'd hit all the squatters. His name, as well as the other names, had been given to Grant by her. A quick search of his mind had not only the adult's name but those of the children as well. Piper even knew how long it had been since the children with two of the families had eaten. It had been a couple of days.

"Mr. Curtain, you don't seem to have taken me seriously. You were told what would happen if you didn't have your things packed up and weren't ready to leave. You're starting to get me in a shitty mood. You don't want that." Mr. Curtain actually pulled his kids in front of him. "Are you going to use your children as a shield, thinking I won't burn you out? That's a very stupid mistake on your part, I'm afraid. You see, I've warned you. After you were warned the other day. This is your final time. Leave, or I will have you burnt out. I can't believe you'd use your children as a way for you to not get harmed. Just so you know, that won't stop us."

"You think anyone is going to serve you with you burning out a man and his kids? Nah, you're the one that is going to be fucked up in all this. My kids and me, we live here. There ain't shit that you can do about it. Now, you get on back to where you came from and leave us alone. We got ourselves a nice place here, and we're going to be living here long after you just start pushing up flowers." Grant asked him if he was threatening him. "No. I know that's against the law. I'm telling you right out, you either leave us alone, all of us, or we're going to hurt you and yours."

The man seemed quite satisfied with his rules against Grant. When Grant laughed, asking her to have a look-see, she hopped down off his shoulder and let her larger bird take her. She stood over Grant by several feet—the man and his children more so. Piper was happy to see Baker ask the kiddies to come on over to him, and they did. It was just the man standing there when Grant asked him once more if he was willing, on his own, to get packed up and go.

"You don't understand what I'm telling you. You

don't have any rights to tell me where I want to live or not. And don't think I'm not going to tell the cops that you took my kids from me." Grant told him he could if he lived. "You're thinking you can kill me, boy? I want you to know I'm not nearly as stupid as you think I am. I got me this here gun, and what do you have? Nothing, I'll tell you, nothing at all."

"I have her." Grant pointed to her, and the man just glanced in her direction. "Doesn't even her size make you think she might well be able to hurt you without much in the way of effort? Your kids are afraid of her."

"Kids are stupid. You can have those two. They ain't worth the trouble anyway. They're forever hungry and wanting something from me. Take'em. I got no use for them. Hell, it'll be nicer here without them." Grant only nodded. "You gonna go away now?"

"No. I'm not. As I have said to you several times now, you're trespassing." The others started toward them. Piper had the feeling this man was the leader of this little group, and he'd bully whoever didn't do things his way. "Do you have your will filled out, Mr. Curtain? Someone we can notify when this is over? Because no matter what you say to the contrary, you're not going to be living here any longer."

"So says you." The man looked at the others. Piper wasn't sure they were thinking Curtain was in the right any longer. Each of them started away once they realized Grant wasn't backing down. "Now look what you've done. You've scared off some of my fine neighbors. I'm afraid now I'm going to have to find me a whole other group of people to piss you off."

"Sorry, but I'm not pissed. I don't get pissed. It's not worth the effort." Grant looked at her and winked. "You see, when you have one of the queen's prey as your mate, you don't have to worry about much of anything bothering you. So this is your final say, is it? You're not moving on?"

"Nope." Curtain aimed his gun at her when she hopped in his direction. Grant told him that if he did that, he was only going to piss her off. "She ain't real anyway."

The gun went off just as she drew in a breath to hit the tent behind the man. As soon as he realized it was flaming, he aimed the gun at Grant. Piper turned her flame to Curtain, and it hit him all at once. Her fire was hotter than anything manmade. Mr. Curtain didn't even have time to scream.

# Chapter 6

The castle was a mix of modern and old. There were places along the walls that would hold things such as books and collections. Grant knew that over the years, he'd collected a lot of both. Mostly books, but he did have a few things he thought would mix well with the things he was sure Piper had collected too. She met him in the office where he was looking around.

"I'm not sure what is going on right now, but the kitchen changes every time I come out and go back into it. I don't cook, you see. I could if pressed, but I don't. So when I leave, it changes, I'm assuming, to your standards of kitchen work. With mine, it's two microwaves, as well as lots of paper plates. I'm not sure I like that." He asked her what was bothering her about it. "That this place is more in tune with me than I am. Do you cook?"

"I do. And I love to. But I think we'll still need

someone here to cook all the time. With the projects we have going, we'll need to do that. Have you heard from Benson about the children?" She told him what she'd heard. "I figured as much. Malnourished seems to be the way children of his sort wind up. Mercy has contacted their mother. She's been looking for them for six months. He took them out of the state when he only had weekend visitation rights. Apparently, she's more than grateful to have them back. The others have left as well. They even cleaned up their messes instead of leaving it for us. I believe you scared some sense into them."

"For the moment anyway." He knew that sometime in the future, they were going to have to do the same again. Grant hoped the castle being occupied would deter some people, but he didn't have much faith. "Baker went to find us some staff. The kitchen is going to be your domain, so you can interview someone for that. I'll see about having the staff here in the morning. I want this night, our first night here, to be just about the two of us. How about we look over the rest of this place, and then we head up to what is going to be our bedroom and make it ours?"

She wiggled her brows at him, and he laughed. Piper was as straight forward as anyone he'd ever met. When she wanted something, Piper didn't have any trouble asking for it. He thought perhaps that was why he loved her so much. Before they went any further, he bent on one knee in front of her.

"It's about time." He laughed again, telling her to behave herself. "I don't know if you've realized this or not, but I don't do behaving very well. I can, I suppose, but what the hell is the fun in all that? But I do love you."

"And I love you. Will you marry me?" Her laughter made him smile. She didn't do ladylike laughter either. When laughing, Piper did so with her entire self. "Is that a yes, or do you have to think on it for a little while?"

"It's very much so a yes. Also, you should know that in all my life, I've never had as much fun as I've had with you these last few days. Thank you for that." He asked her about Curtain. "He was trying to kill you. I know you're immortal and that all he would have done was piss you off. However, he didn't know that. My bird, she didn't want him to harm anyone, and she ended him so we'd not have to watch over our shoulders for the rest of his life. Nor those that he convinced to come here with him. Are you going to put that on my finger, or do I have to do it by myself?"

He pushed the beautiful ring up and over her knuckle. It looked good on her; the ruby was a beautiful gem against her skin. Watching it sparkle all around the room, he nearly missed what she was saying to him. She told him she had one for him as well. When she got down on her knees with him, she put the matching ring on his finger. The ruby was twice the size of hers and set in the same setting he loved on the one he'd given her.

"I had an idea why Jude handed me this yesterday.

She isn't very sneaky, by the way. Don't tell her anything you don't want blabbed around." Piper kissed him and continued. "The rings were a part of a larger set, she told me. There was a necklace, as well as several bracelets in the trunk. Since it had long since rotted, the jewelry had spread out all over the bottom of the sea. I guess Duncan found the rest of it buried under some of the debris that was part of the belly of the ship where the new bride was chained up."

"Such a sad story. I'm sorry." Piper kissed him again, this time lingering a little longer. "You're not upset to have this ring when you know it was for someone that lost everything?"

"No. I mean, I am sorry for the woman that lost her entire family. But I believe you and I can make better, newer stories that go along with this set. We'll be happy. Have children if you want them, as well as live out a long life we can be proud of." She tisked as she continued. "I have a couple of shows coming up at the end of the year. One of them is in Paris, the other in Germany. We'll make a long trip of them if you'd like."

"I would. I would love to see those places with you." She nodded and put her arms over his shoulders. "Anything else before I take you up to our bedroom and ravage you?"

"Yes. I want children with you. By you or not, I want to have little ones running around this place. Bring joy here. Make memories of our lives here that we can be proud of." He told her he liked that idea. "Thank you. Also, I would very much enjoy seeing the world once again, before we get to the point where we're only here all the time. I can see us doing that too. Being people that are so happy with their home, they never want to leave."

"Yes. However, I don't think of you as a homebody. You're more of the kind of woman that goes out and conquers the world one country at a time." They both laughed, and Grant stood up. Scooping Piper up into his arms, he started for the stairs. "It doesn't matter if we're here or abroad; I want to spend my life with you, making you as happy as we can be together."

The bedroom was perfect for them. The bed looked like it was from when he was younger, the wood of it as old as he was. After putting Piper on her feet, he rubbed the post closest to him and could feel the wood speak to him. He turned to Piper when she said his name.

"This is the bed that was in Dante's castle. No one used it, as it was for guests of the household. After the king died, the room this was in was shut off and not used again. It despaired of ever having someone use it again." She asked him if the bed spoke to him. "Not the bed. The wood. Everything has a story to tell. Whether it be old like this or newly cut."

"This is from the stash. I remember seeing it in the corner when we were there last. It called to me, and I remember touching my fingers to the headboard and feeling something. At the time, I thought I had lost my mind. Perhaps it, like this place, knew we'd be here together. Make love to me, Grant. I so need for you to take me." Grant pulled her into his arms and kissed her deeply. "I love you."

She left him there while she went to the bathroom. He wanted to tell her she didn't need to dress up for him. That he wanted only to have her now. However, when she closed the door between them, he could feel his excitement to see what surprise she might have for him.

Pulling the bottle of champagne out of the ice, he wondered where it had come from. Then he remembered Piper had told him she'd asked for something special for their room. He supposed this was their wedding night, and he should have thought of it too. When he heard the door open behind him, Grant turned slowly. Seeing her standing there made his entire body hard as stone.

The glass in his hand shattered from his excitement. Champaign poured down his hand, along with blood from the glass, cutting deeply into his hand. Dropping the bottle to see to his other hand, it hit his bare foot and had him jumping up and down from the pain. He knew what he must look like, but right at that moment, he didn't care. He was hurting. Just as he was getting his shit together and the pain leveling out, he kicked the bottle across the room and hit Piper in the shin. Falling forward to try and catch the projectile, he hit his head on the corner of the bed and laid there. Christ, he thought, I'm a fucking moron. He looked up at Piper when she started laughing.

"Oh my God, Grant, that was by far the funniest thing I've ever witnessed. What the hell happened?" He didn't even bother trying to get up, fearful of what else might befall him. "If I'd not seen this, I would never have believed it. Are you hurt?"

"No. I'm humiliated. Why did you come out of the bathroom naked? Don't you know I'm a man on edge?" He looked up at her again. "Can we start over? And never mention this again? Christ, my head hurts."

Piper got on the floor with him, and he kissed the large knot on her shin. She told him she was just fine but did look at his head. Grant wondered what would have happened had they had a tray of food here too. What sort of mess would he have made then? When she had him sit up, she examined not just his head that had a large knot on it, but also his hand and foot. She was still laughing when she told him he was going to be just fine. Grant pulled her over his lap and held her while she continued to laugh at him.

"Anytime you want to stop laughing is going to be all right with me." That, of course, made her laugh all the harder. "I swear to you, Piper, I've never felt as stupid or as clumsy as I have today. It was as if I'd never seen a naked woman before."

She put her hand over his mouth. "You haven't." He nodded and kissed the palm of her hand. "Also, just so you know, neither have I seen a naked man. We're new to each other. All right?" She laughed a little more. "Of course, if you were to tell me you'd really not seen a naked woman before, I'd believe you, after that show of clumsiness."

"Yes, well, I wasn't expecting you to be naked." He kissed her neck, then her shoulder. "Perhaps we should stay on the floor, so I don't toss you across the room when I enter you. You never know."

"I do know. I know you're the best thing that has ever happened to me." She turned on his lap, so she was facing him. Grant willed his clothing away, and she hummed at him. "Very nice, Mr. Coby. You have wonderfully warm skin."

They touched each other. Smoothed their fingers over their skin. Massaged muscles. Grant tasted her nipples, her entire breast. He even suckled on her ear lobes. Tasting each part of her that he could, Grant was getting a wonderful idea that his mate was as beautiful naked as she was in clothes.

Lifting her up when she asked for help, Grant slid Piper down over his cock like she'd been made to be there. He didn't move, didn't touch her again while he held his breath and counted to ten. Then to twenty. As soon as she moved, her body adjusting to his, he put his hands on her arms and held her still. When she giggled, he looked into her face.

"You're very large." He nodded, not sure he could speak over the large knot in his throat. "I love the way you feel inside of me, Grant. Like you're now a part of me forever."

Rolling over, so she was under him, he cried out when her legs wrapped around his hips. Not in pain, but in pure pleasure. Again he didn't move, trying his best not to come yet. He'd never been so close to coming even when he'd been with his first woman. Piper put her hands on his face and pulled him down for a long and very thorough kiss.

"You're very beautiful. Too much for me, almost." She grinned at him and moved her hips. "Christ, do you have any idea what you're doing to me?"

"Yes." She moved again, this time raising her hips up to meet his downward stroke. It was too much for him and not nearly enough. "Take me, Grant. Please? I need to have you fill me."

Wanting to take his time made him pause. When she moved again, he held her hips still as he looked into her eyes. Then, just like that, it occurred to him that he'd have the rest of his life with this woman. He'd be able to make love to her whenever he wanted. Have a quickie in the yard or even a long bath with her in the house. She was his. Forever and a day.

"I love you, Piper. For the rest of my days, I will love you more and more." He laid his head on her forehead and smiled. "You are the very best part of me."

Grant made love to her. He touched every inch of her that he could reach. Tasted parts of her body that were made for him. Even as he filled her over and over with his cock, he told her with words and actions how much he needed her in his life. How he wanted her there for him. But mostly just how much he loved her.

Piper's nipples were peaked, and he couldn't resist suckling at them. Her fingers wove through his hair and massaged his scalp. It was strangely erotic the way she touched him there. Even when he held her tighter to his body, he could see places on her flesh that he'd missed. More places to explore. When she came, shouting out his name and her love for him, Grant joined her, coming down to earth with the only woman he'd ever love.

~*~

Piper left their bedroom just as the sun was coming up. They'd made love several times throughout the night, and she was sore in places she'd never realized existed before. Moving down the steps, she had to smile. Getting the better of Grant had been more fun than she thought it might be.

He'd gotten up to go to the bathroom. Time had ceased to mean anything to the two of them. For all she knew, it could well have been several days or only several minutes since they'd dragged themselves to bed. But she wanted him again and had followed him into the bathroom. He was washing his hands just as she entered.

Sitting up on the counter, she spread her legs wide for him. Touching her fingers to her nipples made her hum with pleasure. That was all it took for him to attack her right then and there. He'd fucked her hard enough that the sink would never be the same. The floor had also suffered greatly.

Now she had to get to work. The idea that had been playing around in her head all day yesterday had finally come to fruition. She knew not only what it would look like, but what she wanted to use—glass and metal. It was something she'd wanted to play with for a while, but the project for it had never been there. Now it was.

"Mistress?" The little faerie was sitting atop one of her flames. It wasn't on, thankfully, but she did warn him that should it have just been turned off, he'd still be hurt. "Thank you for that. I'll warn the others. We have something to ask of you. Should you say no, we would continue to stay here in your domain. The master of the house, he said we were to ask you for whatever we wanted, as this is your place of peace."

"He's correct. However, I don't mind that any of you are here. For some reason, I have more peace when I know someone is in here with me." She asked him what he wanted. "However, if you want heat or air, it's coming soon. The furnace, as well as the air conditioner, is going to be installed next month. The insulation and the vents are already here, so it won't take them long to install it."

"That is most excellent, my lady. Most excellent indeed. What we were wishing to ask you about is if you could please leave the water on for us. While we can go out and get it should we want, some of the others here, they're breeding and do not wish to leave their young ones." She told him she thought faeries were born in the flowers. "Most are. A great many of them are yearly. But these are our children. The ones that will take over the other jobs we have, such as the building of furniture. Some of the houses we use are needed for those couples."

"I didn't know that. I thank you for the information. In addition to the water being left on for you, is there anything else that I can do for you? I noticed that you've found the sugar cubes I've left out for you, as well as the petals. I have to admit, I wouldn't have thought of either of those without Grant telling me. I had no idea what I thought you'd do for food in here, but I'm sorry it took me so long to put them out for you." The little man told her they had ways of getting in and out of the building. However, *it was* difficult. She heard the tone he had but chose to ignore it for now. "Is there anything else I can do for you?"

"The scraps that you leave behind. We've been collecting them to use for things such as knives and the like. We were wondering if you'd show us how to use the sanding thing over there so that we might be able to make them sharper, or even bend them in a way to make other utensils." She followed him across the room, terrified that he wanted to use her electric sander. All sorts of things jumbled around in her head until she thought of something else. She stopped in her tracks. "My lady?"

"This wasn't here yesterday. This building was...

it's just like the one I had at home, but attached to the house as—" She looked around. "It's much bigger than the one I had at home. This is new too. I just realized that everything in here is brand new." He nodded at her, looking at her like she was off her noddle. Perhaps she was. "You were in the other building I was using. I saw you there. Where did this come from?"

"I did it." She turned and looked at Grant when he came into the door. "I told you I had magic of my own. And being fae, I could ask the earth for all kinds of things. This, however, is a duplication of the other building you had. Only, as you pointed out, much larger. I wanted you to be happy here. I would have been happy too if you'd not left so early this morning."

She laughed and kissed him as he had her. They had company, and she didn't want to get into this with him while the others were wanting answers. Taking his hand, she went to the other side of the room with the little man. The first thing she wanted to know was his name.

"Gosh, I completely forgot. My name is Key, my lady. 'Tis an odd name, I'm told, but I like the way it sounds when I say it. Key." There were several sanders in the area he'd taken them to. One of them was the very one she had been afraid of him using. However, all he wanted to know how to use was the sandpaper. "It would be easy for us to use, I think, but it's much too large for us to carry around. If you'd show us how to use it, we'd be very grateful."

"You tell me how big of a piece you're wanting to use, Key, and I'll cut some of this up for you. Also, you should know that there are different grades of it. Some is used for shaping, but I also have the kind of sandpaper that is used for making the surface smooth. I'll cut you up some of all that I have. When you need more, you need only to tell me. I'll gladly do this for you."

As she and Grant helped cut up the paper with scissors, they talked about the building. The others, perhaps a dozen or so more little people, came to help, carrying the cut paper to a place that would be out of her way. Piper decided to make them an area all of their own, so they could have their own space.

Grant put together some cardboard boxes for them, smaller than anything a person could ship in, but perfect for the faeries. They even brought down some of the things they'd been making with her scraps, and she was pleased to see that they'd made tables and chairs with some of it.

Piper was delighted with the things they were making and told them that if they wished, she'd give them more metal and items in the building for them to use for the others around. They even hung up some of the little suncatchers they'd made from broken glasses and bottles they'd found.

"I think you've made yourself some very good friends." She looked at Grant and smiled. She told him how much she liked them being there. "Yes, I can understand that. What you have here are the older faeries. Even some of them older than us. They're not put out to pasture as humans would do to older beings, but they find themselves something to do, as you have given them the tools for, and barter what they make for things that others make. These little people will be the envy of every other faerie in the land."

"Once, just a few years ago, I had a piece that went to a greenhouse. They were huge at the time, and while I was waiting for the check they owed me, I had a look around. There were these little gardens in the dirt. I remember thinking that while I know only a very few faeries, I couldn't see them putting out all the crap the humans thought they'd have." He asked her what was there. "Well, for one thing, they had these toadstools in bright, colorful colors. That just screamed, come and find me. Also, they had swing sets and grills. Why on earth would a faerie need a grill? They don't eat meat, nor do they usually grill their flowers. Also, and this was something I just simply could not wrap my head around, they had gardens. Some of the seeds would have been ten times the size of the faerie. Not to mention, how on earth would they have been able to plant more than one thing? Humans have such an odd sense of things."

They were still laughing when she started to work on her newest project. Grant talked to her about the things he had to look into, and she sort of half heard him. At some point, he kissed her on the cheek and left. Piper wouldn't have been able to tell you anything he'd said to her when he left or if she'd said anything to him. This work was all she could concentrate on right now.

Grant brought her lunch. She was sure she ate at least some of it. Her belly wasn't growling as it usually did when she was working. Stepping back from the piece she'd been thinking about, her heart did a little jump. Piper had to keep telling herself she'd made this, and it wasn't something she'd picked up. It was, to her, the most beautiful piece she'd ever made.

It was a water feature; she thought they called it. The metal stand stood about six feet tall and had two dozen branches all around it. The branches she'd put there were hollow, so the water could slowly flow out of them into the beautiful colored cups at the tip of each branch. She was almost afraid to turn it on, fearing it wasn't going to work. Or worse yet, it wouldn't be nearly as beautiful as she thought it would be. She wanted Grant to see it first.

*Can you come out here please? I need you to see something.* He asked her if she was all right. *Yes. Just finished this, and I wanted you to see if it works with me. Unless you're busy. I can understand that.*

*No, I'm not busy.* He laughed. *Do you have any idea how long you've been out there, love?* She told him a few hours, at least. *You've been there for three days. Three days. I talked to Remi about it, and she said I shouldn't bother you, but to take you food out once in a while and make sure it was close enough for you to find. Then I was to leave. Right now, it's three in the morning. I'm on my way.*

*No. It can wait.* Grant told her it couldn't. He wanted to see it as well. *I'm so sorry about this. I had no idea. I've done this before, but I've usually been the only one that would be worried about me eating. I can't wait for you to see this. I hope it turns out all right.*

Grant smiled at her from the doorway. As he made his way to her, she noticed that he did look like he'd just gotten out of bed, and she hated even more that she had bothered him. He assured her that it was wonderful that she wanted him to come out.

"I've hooked up the water to it. I'm not sure how I did that, as I've never done anything like this before. But I guess I know enough." Piper asked Grant to turn the water on. "But step back, so it doesn't fall on you if it's wrong."

The water coming through the tubes was starting to spurt and make noises. Just as she was ready to turn it off, Grant told her to wait. There would be air in the lines. As the water began to reach the highest level, it started to flow over the glass cups just as she had imagined it.

"Piper, this is wonderful. The water, as it comes out, blends in with the glass perfectly. It reminds me of dew on the grass in the morning." The sound was also just as she imagined it would be. Like the trickling stream they'd all played in as birds while with Dante. "This is magnificent. Thank you so much for sharing this with me first. I cannot believe how lovely this is. I hope you plan to put it in our front yard. This would be such an amazing piece of work."

She was giddy with excitement. The fact that he loved it as much as she did only made her more excited to see what else she could do with working for her own pleasure. Glancing over at the birds she was doing, Piper knew she had only one more bird to do, and that was of herself. Even the castle was finished up.

"What is going on with this piece?" She walked over to where he was. There was a line that she'd been working on. The metal hadn't been working the way she wanted it to, she told him. "What was the plan? Because I can see this working in a couple of things I have going right now. Remember me telling you about the things in my trunk? There were several tapestries that I would love to hang. If you'd not mind, I can make these into the perfect hangers."

"Sure. I can even decorate the ends of them should you want. The ends will need to be fixed so that the hanging item doesn't fall off the rod." She picked up the longest one at about three feet. "These would work out well for them too, as they won't rust or make any sort of marks on them. Thanks. I didn't want to have to toss these out, and I love that idea."

Grant told her what other things were in his trunk. When they made their way into the house, he showed her some of the things he didn't understand. The book, handmade and full of recipes, was perfect for him. Dante had made her mate feel as much a part of her family as she had them all those years ago.

She knew that Dante had sewn some of the tapestries. They were scenes of the castle, crudely done, but lovely enough for them to hang. Piper had noticed that they had windows with glass in them in all the rooms. The addition that had been put on the right side held not only several bedrooms but also a place she thought would be perfect for children to play. The way it was filled with soft carpet, a fireplace, as well as a great many windows also had her thinking that the room would also make a nice room for family gatherings, like Thanksgiving and Christmas.

Here it was only June, and she was ready to put up Christmas again. Shaking her head, she helped Grant hang not just the tapestries but also the other paintings that Dante had wanted him to have.

There was one Piper loved more than the others. It was a painting of the six of them sitting on a fenceline someplace. As their small birds, they were lined up in order of being changed. After her were Remi and Esme. Piper had hopes that they'd find their mates soon. It was wonderful having someone around you all the time that didn't annoy the shit out of you. Laughing to herself, she did wonder what Grant would say if she told him her thoughts on having him around. He'd more than likely tell her the same about her being around. She so loved this man.

By the time they finished putting up the things from the trunk, the two of them were starving. It was still early morning, and she realized it had been a while since she'd eaten. Once she decided she was hungry, Piper thought she could eat an entire vat of seeds. Settling on a bowl of cereal while Grant fixed them something more substantial, Piper thought of the other things she needed to get done before she went to bed tonight.

Right now, she thought she might not make it another hour. Once her belly was filled, all Piper wanted to do was nap. Lying down on the couch while Grant read the recipes he'd gotten, Piper was asleep in no time.

# *Chapter 7*

The things that had been brought up from the underwater graveyard were beginning to fill up the large barn that had been put up to hold it all. Not only had they been able to find several large trunks of coins, but there had been a great many swords as well. Piper had been able to get them looking good again with her heat. Remi had used a sword at one time in her life. Being a pirate with the others had been fun too. Pulling one of them from the scabbard that had also been found with them, she played with it for several minutes before she realized she was no longer alone.

"I didn't see you there." Grant told her it was all right, that he'd been coming here to do the same thing. "I used to be really good at one of these. But after all this time, all I can do is mimic the moves. I'd never be able to survive if I had to defend myself with one again. How about you?"

"I had several of these at one time. I thought of myself as a collector of all things violent. That period of my life only lasted long enough for my mom to have found them. I think I was all of ten at the time. But the queen, Dante, she gave me one when I was a little older. And she left me one in my trunk." Remi told him she had some too. And that she too had a trunk for her mate. "She was a very generous person. I wish I'd known her as well as you guys did."

"I remember one time when we were all away from the castle. I never really minded being away from the people there. But I was able to have a little fun with being a bird of prey. I guess having to fend for myself back then made me realize how much I depended on the others for help. The queen, she needed us all, not just one of us, to help her. Not that she was cruel to me or anything, but being a vulture, I'm not exactly the most beautiful bird around." He said he had seen her and thought she was. "Thanks for that. No, you have the most beautiful of all of us. Piper has color and vibrance that none of the rest of us have. I love her, don't get me wrong, but I'm very jealous of her beauty too."

"You're very beautiful, Remi. The silver of your hair with the green of your eyes mesmerized me from the beginning." Not that she was vain, but she did glance in the mirror that had been found in the sea with other women's things. "The way your hair glistens in the moonlight is one of the most breathtaking things I've ever witnessed."

"Now you're just being mean." He said he was serious. "I do hope that when I find my mate, he is as sweet and strong as you are, Grant. You're so calm and nice. Even when you're mad, as I've seen in you with people when they're not doing what they should, you still look like you couldn't have chocolate melt in your mouth. In the event you didn't know this about me, chocolate is one of my biggest downfalls when it comes to sweets."

"Yours and Duncan's. I heard that the other day he nearly ate an entire ten pound box of the sweets. Me? I don't really get into really super sweet things. I like apples and other fruit." She made fun of him again about being a purest. "I guess I am. I just enjoy what the earth gives me. Probably the fae in me."

"No, I'd say it was the niceness in you." She looked at the swords and then back at him. "Want to play around a little? I'm sure we can both have some fun with them before anyone finds us."

"Absolutely."

He took one of the larger swords, and Remi watched as he tested its weight. None of them were cheaply made. Several of them had been made with the king in mind, she'd bet. There were so many jewels on a couple of them she knew that they were for show only and not for real use. When Grant had one that he said he could work with, they started working the room, wielding the swords like she was sure he had long ago.

By the time she was too exhausted to lift her arm, she was covered in sweat, and her hair was sticking to her head. Remi was glad she'd been able to get in a few digs, and Grant had done a good job on her as well. There were cuts on her flesh as well as her clothing. She found that she didn't care. It had been that much fun.

"I'd like to spar with you again sometime. I feel out of shape right now, but I think this would go a long way in helping me out. It's a damned sight better than walking." She said he should fly. That took a lot of muscle movements. "You know, I forgot about that. That I could fly. I'll have to talk to Piper about it when she gets back."

"Where did she go? We have dinner together every Wednesday night. She's never missed one before." He told her what he knew. "I can see that. She'll make it then. Those fires, I think they take a great deal out of her when she has to have someone arrested. The fire that she went to last week. What do you know about it? If I can ask."

"Sure, you can. It was arson. The number of bodies that were in the place is going to mean hard time for the two men that caused the fire. Piper not only found out who had done it but their reasoning behind it. Not that their reasons are sound ones, but she did find them." Remi asked him what she'd found out. "They were fired the week before. They figured they'd just fire everyone in the place because of them not having a job. I don't think they thought anyone would be in the place on a Saturday morning. That's the morning they do a deep cleaning of the place, and it caught a lot of people inside."

"Did Piper tell you she's been to several fires that took a lot of lives? Believe it or not, she hates it. It was why I was so surprised she took this job with the Feds. She can pick up the reason something burned to the ground in no time. It's dealing with the aftermath of one, the bodies or insurance, that really gets her upset. I'm betting that before too much longer, she has to quit. It's very hard on her."

"I'll keep an eye on her for it then. Thank you for the heads up." Remi told him it was her pleasure. "She's been working in her studio nonstop for the last few weeks. I think that since someone told her that she didn't have to do pieces that people wanted to see and could do what she wanted, she's taken that to heart. Some of the pieces she has finished are spectacular. Work like I'm betting no one has seen before."

"She told me about the water tower. I can't wait to see it. Did I tell you she sometimes comes and helps me out at the restaurants? It's not that big of a deal for her, but when I need something cooked really hot and fast, she lends me her breath. I can't tell you how many times she's saved my ass." The two of them laughed at that. "She's my favorite of all my sisters. I'm sure the others love her too, but not like I do. Piper has been my rock and my foundation so many times that I can't count them all."

"I'm sure you've been there for her as well." Remi told him she had, but not in the way that Piper had been for her. "I can see the closeness between the two of you sometimes. Mercy loves you all, but she's more standoffish about it. Jude, she's quiet about her love. You know it's there, and you love her for it, but she's the gentle one of the six of you. Not that she couldn't be hard when necessary, but it's in her nature to use her voice rather than violence to take care of something. Esme. She's a little harder to read. A loner for sure. Her anger or whatever she's dealing with comes out in her paintings and art. The colors mostly are what tells me she is angry. It's not on her face or the makeup of her body, but it's in her work." She asked him about her. "You've been the most difficult of all of them to pinpoint. Mostly I think it's because I don't see you as often. You've been gone more than here since you've all moved to this area. You're generous. I have discovered that. Twice in the last two weeks, I was going to help out Benson and my mom and found that it was already finished up. I found out that you've been doing that with all the people around here. I particularly love that you've made sure the grade school has new buses for the kids."

"I have no idea what you might be talking about." Grant laughed. "I'll thank you not to tell anyone what you know. They think I'm selfish. I'm sort of liking that for now. But the buses, they were needed, and I had the means to get them with very little effort on my part."

"No one thinks you're selfish. And you'd be surprised at the fact that Piper knows what you're up to. She is jealous at times that you're quick at getting things done before she even hears about it." Remi smiled at him. "Ah. I see. You do that on purpose. Good for you. It keeps her on her toes. The rest of them as well. I'm sure you know already, but what are your plans for your share of the hidden treasures? You have it all mapped out, I'm betting."

"I do—at least a portion of it. I'm going to open a place that will serve meals to those in need. I'm calling it Pay it On. Pay as you can afford it. And if you can afford two meals, the money will go toward someone that can't afford a meal." Grant told her that was a nice idea. "Thanks. I already have one opening in the worst part of Ohio. I'm hoping to use it as a model for a few more. It's not my idea, but I'm expanding on someone else's. I think it's about the best way I can help feed the hungry."

They talked about other projects the two of them were heading up. Remi knew how to cook and enjoyed it. That alone was what helped her a great deal in feeding the masses with not much in the way of money. It seemed that Grant had a few ideas concerning helping the underprivileged.

"When I was younger—even now, actually—there was always food on our table. Meat too, even though we didn't eat all that much of it. I did figure out after a few years that if we were having meat, that meant my mom had invited someone to the house to get a hot meal. There wasn't much in the way of poverty around here, thanks to Dante. But there were a few older people that had no one to help them out. No family." Remi asked about the kitchen that had been set up. "That was a wonderful idea that Dante had. Having a kitchen cooking meals all day long for those in need. However, if a person wasn't able to get to the kitchen, it did them little good. My mom tried to have meals delivered to them a few times, but as I got busier with school and such, it was more and more difficult for either of us to make sure everyone was fed. Not that it was anyone's fault that these people didn't have food every meal, but someone should have checked on them. That's what I'm doing in larger cities. I have a group of older, but not elderly, people going door to door in the older areas and seeing what they can do for the shut ins. Not only does it get the people traveling a good meal, but they fix meals for the elderly person that they can reheat when needed. All of it is made in their home and with their things. It makes them feel safer, I believe."

"I love that. Yes, I can see that. I'm guessing these people, they'll pick up things for them as well?" Grant told her that the only thing they couldn't pick up was meds. "Why not medication? I mean, that would seem to me as a perfect thing for them to do."

"I have heard where groups of people will *say* that they're helping the elderly by picking up things for them. Using their credit card or cash to go and get things like food and picking up their meds when they're ready. Then when their bills come in, the person is gone with their medications and has been buying groceries for their own home instead of the person they're working for. Medications, some of them, anyway, have a high resell value. I'd rather not have to have them go without medications over food anytime." Remi thought perhaps this was something that not only had Grant heard about but had experience with too. "When necessary, there will be a car driven by a pharmacist that will take their medications to them. While there, he or she can explain what it is they're taking, as well as any kind of side effects they might experience."

"Does Piper know how wonderful you are?" Grant's face pinked up; embarrassment looked adorable on him. "If you ever feel underappreciated, you come and see me. A nice handsome man like you is good to have around."

He left her there then. Remi was still laughing about his hasty exit while she put some of the things that had been brought in today away. It had been her job to catalog and mark everything they brought here. Soon, she knew, they'd have to start looking for a larger place. At least one that would hold a few dozen shelves, as they were bringing the smaller things up now.

As she emptied the last of the carts, she turned and looked at some of the things they'd been able to save. Most of the material and soft goods might well have been destroyed. But thanks to the magic that Grant had, a few of the dresses and some of the men's clothing had been brought up with no issues. She knew that on other finds like this one, they would have been completely destroyed. However, magic had made it so everything was as nice and new as it had been when the ship was boarded. Remi hoped they'd put them in a museum someplace nearby. She was sure that others would love to see the sort of dress that was popular back then for the rich and stupid. Remi was sure they'd think of a different title for them, but hers was more appropriate.

Leaving the warehouse, she locked up and headed back to the dock. Piper was coming her way with some more things to sort. It was going to be a long while before this stuff could be divided up. Remi was looking forward to using a few of the pieces in her new home. She only hoped that if she ever had a mate, he'd like what she had. Or he could just leave. At this point in her life, Remi could take a man or leave him. It no longer seemed important to her to have a man around all the time.

~*~

Piper walked around the cave twice before she found the things she'd been looking for. Looking at her list, she had a long way to go before she was finished up. They had each remembered something they wanted her to look for. One of the things was the harness that the queen rode on when flying upon Mercy's back. She knew where she'd seen it last, so headed in that direction. Grant came from one of the many smaller caves with his arms loaded down with things too. Piper went to help him.

"I should have figured I'd find things I'd like to take back with us." Piper asked him what he'd found. "Well, I did find that picture of the seascape that we were to look for. It's very well done. Do you know who the signature is?"

"Yes. If you look at it closely, you can make it out too." Grant picked up the framed painting and held it close to his face. Finally, when he got it, he looked at her. "I had no idea why he never took it out of here in the first place. It's a wonderful work of art. I'm sure if you were to look for that name there, he's been painting like that forever. Who would have thought that Duncan would sign his work DHQD? But if you know what his middle name is, it makes sense. Duncan Harrison, Son of Queen Dante."

"He's really good. Even as old as I believe this is, Duncan really was quite the painter." She told him there were more, but she'd not been able to locate them. "I think I have a couple of smaller paintings of his. They were marked for me to sell them for the cash for unknown projects. I have a feeling, however, that she knew just what projects they would be used for. Don't you?"

"Dante could see the future in bits and pieces, I found out later. I have no idea how extensive they were. However, Duncan told me that she gave him a list of companies to buy up and when to sell them off. It's what kept him from ever running out of money to keep the town surviving." He asked her if that was legal. "I'm not sure it could be insider trading since she gave him the information well before the companies were made. I mean, I think that would be why it's not illegal."

"You're more than likely right. I never thought of the companies not even existing yet." Grant laughed a little. "Well, I guess we should finish up here. I have plans to take you as many ways I can think of tonight."

"Why must we wait?" She moved toward him and hoped she was making a good move. "I would love nothing more than to take your cock into my mouth and suck you down my throat."

"Christ, woman. The things that come out of your mouth."

Piper bent in front of him and unbuttoned his jeans. He didn't say anything more, but she could read his face and see that he was needy.

Taking his cock out of his pants, she heard his sharp inhale of breath as she wrapped her hand around his thickness, watching Grant's face. Kissing the tip, she moaned when his cock leaked onto her lips. Taking him into her mouth, she knew this was the way a man should be made love to.

His cock was thick and long. She couldn't swallow all of him past her tight throat, but he seemed to be enjoying what she was able to. As she fondled his balls, making sure they had as much attention as she was giving his cock, Grant wrapped his hand into her hair and held her still. Piper wasn't having any of that.

Letting his cock go, she licked him from root to tip. Lingering over the crown of him, she tickled the opening several times before he cried out enough. Piper wanted to make him come all over her. To mark her in a way that she'd never forget when coming to the cave. As soon as she was able to squeeze his balls, none too gently, he came so hard he nearly smothered her with his hot juices. It was enough to make her come too, screaming out his name as she tried to catch every drop of his cum.

Before she could figure out his intentions, he picked her up and slammed her over his cock. The cool wall of the cave touched her back. The contrast to his too hot body with the cool stone on her back had her begging him to fill her. Grant fucked her hard, harder than he had before. As soon as he came, throwing back his head with it, she came with him.

It was epic, coming this way. Holding onto him so that she'd not break apart, Piper begged for more. When Grant bit her on the shoulder, Piper screamed from the pain, then the pleasure of it. The man was going to kill her, she was sure of it. Then she simply blacked out.

When she woke, she was lying on some of the material that had been stored in here. Piper could hear Grant; he was whistling a tune that she thought was as old as he was. Dressing herself, she felt the pull of several muscles as they stretched. She would have thought she was in better shape. However, there were no exercises one could do to prepare for making love like they had. Standing up, she held onto the wall as her body pulled even more.

"You should play with some of the swords we have at home." She looked at him and growled. "I'm assuming you don't think that's funny. However, I think you're simply the most beautiful woman I've ever met when you do that."

"You're nuts." He laughed and laid some of the things from his hands on the floor beside her. After kissing her, he started to walk back to where he'd been. "Wait. What does swordplay have to do with being sore?"

"Remi and I have been playing around with the swords for the last few days. It's an amazing workout. She's getting better daily. I'm just glad I can't be killed." Piper wasn't even jealous that Remi was with her mate. "Remi said that at one time, all six of you were pirates. I would love to hear some of the stories about that."

"None of the rest of us liked it as much as Remi did. But we stayed with her until we found other things to do. We weren't the only female pirates, as we first thought. More and more women took to the seas to help their families. For us, it was just a way to help with the boredom." He asked her what they had gathered from the ships. "Mostly slaver ships were our targets. We'd return most of them to wherever they'd been taken from. A lot of them were happy just to have meals and water. They would stay on board with us until they could get their own ship and help us. For a long time, it was the only source of income we had. It was a learning experience, if nothing else."

As she loaded the things they'd gathered onto one of the many barge like carriers that they'd used long ago, she told Grant about all the things she'd noticed that needed to be taken care of in town. First and foremost, she thought they needed to have more jobs. Most of the younger people would leave New Town to find work.

"I've been thinking about that too. Mom told me that someone has to travel all the way to the next town to get things to plant. Of course, my mom and I were planting the same seeds over and over because of what we are." Piper asked him if he meant a greenhouse. "Yes. Not only that but also a few other department like stores. Nothing huge — I think that would take away from the quietness of the town. But a hardware store would be nice. Perhaps even a fresh garden place. Things that people can bring in and sell so that others can have a bit of the things they've not grown. Also, I've been thinking about two more projects. What would you say to having sheep in our keep? Not just sheep, but animals that would take care of the lawns without having to mow. I'm not saying we'll never mow, but they can be a source of fertilizer as well as meat when they're too old."

"I believe at one time, Dante had that going on. But back then, meat was much more important and not readily available as it is now. I like that idea. I also think that what you said about fertilizer is good. Natural is the way to go, I think." Grant thanked her and then told her of his second idea. "An online auction weekly? What sort of things do you think we could put on there? I'm all willing to have our little town profitable, but I don't know what anyone would want to buy."

"I was thinking of Key and the things he was telling us about the faerie gardens. The little things that they make, we could put them up for sale. Then, in turn, buy more seeds for them to plant. That would not only be profitable, but it would help them with foodstuffs as well." She nodded, thinking of all the things they could sell off with the things from the downed ship. Piper told him about it. "That's a perfect idea. No one would have to come here to see what they're buying. Putting it online too will have millions of people looking at the treasures, as well as having an opportunity to buy things they'd not be able to usually."

"We'd have to run it by the rest of the family." He said he'd not have it any other way. "Good. You know, we have a great deal of things in here that I think none of us want or need. Not to say that we should just get rid of it. But Dante did want us to sell some of it off for just that reason. A way to keep the town from going under."

As they stacked the things they were taking back on the two barges, they traded ideas on other projects. Piper was glad that Grant took them running the castle seriously. She did as well, but it was difficult for her to figure out how to get people to come there to live. Grant said he'd speak to Duncan about it. He was the only king he knew.

"Me too, now that I think about it."

After Piper showed Grant how to carry his load, he lifted up in the air. He was doing much better than anyone else when it came to flying. Jude thought it was because he was fae, who had known how to fly long before she'd been hatched. Picking up her load, she followed him back to their home. Most of the things being brought back were for the other households, but a few pieces, mostly furniture, were for their home. She'd picked up the two bedframes that she'd been thinking about for one of the many bedrooms in their home.

*Where the hell are you?* She asked Mercy why she was screaming at her. *I'm having this baby. Come to me before I have to test not being able to hurt my mate and kill him. He's driving me insane. You'd think he'd never had a baby before.*

*He didn't.* After telling Mercy she was on her way, she reminded Mercy that Joel was a father because he'd not known about her as a baby. *Miley was already born when he got her.*

*I don't care. He's making me crazy here.* She landed on the front lawn of Mercy's home and told her sister she was there. *Tell Grant I want him to take Joel on a long walk off a very short pier. Seriously, it's not even that bad yet. He's acting like I'm on my last breath here.*

*Because he loves you.* Mercy snorted. *Well, he does. Why? I haven't any idea. You're a sourpuss and mean. I swear, there are times when I think you should have your mouth washed out with soap.*

Piper and Grant took the stairs up to Mercy's room. Grant did end up taking Joel away. The two seconds she was in the room with him, she could understand Mercy's issue. The man was a little bonkers.

"What is it you want me to do?" Mercy moved back the covers that Joel had put over her and handed Piper the baby. "You've had her? Well, that sucks. Why didn't you say so?"

"There's more. If Joel would have known that, I would never have gotten rid of him. This little bit was difficult enough without scaring Joel into having a heart attack. The man was about to bounce off the walls." Not sure what she meant, Piper's heart jumped when Mercy cried out with pain again that there were going to be twins. "The second baby is ready to be born. I'm so glad you're here with me."

It didn't take long for the second, then the third child to be born. A daughter, then a son, and another daughter in order of birth. Their magic was strong, Piper knew. All three of them were going to be powerful beings. After cleaning them up, the babies were laid on the big bed with their mom.

"Joel is going to be such a good dad. Don't you think?" Piper told Mercy she thought so as well. "I love him so much. And now I have three little ones that we'll share. Miley is going to love it."

"I'm sure she will. Where is she, anyway? I'd have thought you wanted her in here with you." She looked away. "What is it, Mercy? Why isn't she here with you today?"

"We had a fight. Not really a fight, but a disagreement on her being able to date. I said no, but she went to her father, and he said it was all right." Piper asked her why he would allow her to date. "It's not a real date, I found out later, but a bunch of her friends meeting for pizza. I swear to you, she never told me that part. That's when she told me I was mean to her, and she was never speaking to me again."

"May I fix this?" Mercy cried. Hard sobs that made her own heart hurt with it. "Mercy, I'm going to fix this. I promise you. I'll have her come to tell you how sorry she is too."

"Don't force her into anything." She said that she'd not. "The only reason I'm letting you do this is because I'm feeling too emotional to talk to her right now. I so wanted her here when I— Oh, Piper, she hurt my heart so badly."

Piper held onto her sister as she cried. This was a side of Mercy she'd never experienced before. Reaching out to Grant to tell him that Joel could come in, she also told him what she was going to do next. All he said to her was not to kill the little girl.

*I'm not able to, remember?* He said that didn't mean she'd not try. *Yes, I might try. I'll be around later. I'm talking to her right now.*

# Chapter 8

Piper didn't bother asking to see Miley but just looked for her. When she found her down at the dock, watching the boats coming in for the day, Piper sat down beside her. She was ready to blast her when she spoke first.

"I ruined everything, Aunt Piper. Not only that, but I'd not be the least bit surprised if Mom sends me off to military school after what I did yesterday." Piper told her that Mercy was crying when she'd left her. "I don't know what's wrong with me anymore. I fight against everything. Even if she told me to do my homework, something I love to do, I'd just not do it because she told me to do it. Now, I'm sitting out here with no idea how I fix this."

"Do you want to?" Miley just stared at her. "I think that is a good question. Do you want to continue to sit out here feeling sorry for yourself, or do you really want to fix this? Because from what I was told, you were a fucking bitch to the woman that not only healed you but also took you to her heart. That isn't a way to get on any of our good sides."

"She's all I ever wanted in a mom. I have everything I could ever want from her too. Not just material things. I mean love, and she loves my dad too. Mom loves my dad, and now they're going to have a baby. They're so happy." Piper didn't mention that the babies had been born. She'd tell her later, she thought. "Getting ready for the new one coming, Mercy has tried her best to get me involved. And you have no idea how much I wanted to be. But a part of me felt betrayed that they're going to all this trouble for them."

"You think they didn't do anything for you?" Miley just shrugged her shoulders. Piper gave her a hard slap to her face, and Miley held her cheek and started crying. "What the fuck? You cannot just sit there and tell me that Mercy didn't bend over backwards for you. Even after she was tossed out of your father's home, she continued to help you. That's not even talking about her healing you. Christ, I should just let you sit here until you rot. To think that I was so excited to have lunch with you sometime soon." Piper stood up. "If it's anything at all to you, your...no, Mercy has given birth. While you sit here on your ass, shrugging off how you think she helped you, she's sobbing her fucking eyes out because you weren't there when it all occurred. You should be beaten."

Piper shifted and took to the skies. It was in her to go and shit on the girl's head. Flying as far from her as possible while still being able to keep an eye on her, Piper landed outside the home of Benson and Molly. She wanted to talk to Molly in the worst sort of way.

Molly was the mother she'd never had. Not that she even remembered a time when she'd had a mom, but Piper had been going to her regularly over the last few weeks. As soon as she was let into the house, Molly told her to come into the kitchen, then smacked her on the back of the head when she was seated.

"What was that for?" She told her that she had spoken to Miley. "I did. But I don't understand how that is deserving of a pop to the back of my head."

"Would you like another pop?" Shaking her head, Piper told her what had happened. "I'm going to allow this of you this one and only time. Because you don't know. You and the others have no idea what it's like for a teenager. Miley is going through something that none of you have experienced, nor will you ever. She's changing daily. Her heart is taking a beating too. Teenagers, humans and shifters alike go through this sort of thing all the time. They're not mean. They're confused. I'm sure you didn't help matters one bit by making her cry."

"She hurt Mercy." She said that Mercy was next on her list. "This is insane. I came here to talk to you, and you're yelling at me. I don't like that."

She hit her again. "Listen to me. Or better yet, reach

out to that little girl and tell me what you're feeling from her." She did and was astonished to hear that Miley was as depressed as she'd ever felt a person to be. "That's not entirely on you, but a great deal of it is. Lucky for you that I love you, or I wouldn't have helped all of you out. When you have trouble with someone, do you accuse or ask questions first?"

"So that you don't hit me again, you tell me the answer to that." Piper was beginning to hate the fact that she'd come here when Molly hit her anyway. "What the fuck am I supposed to do?"

"You reach out for help. I'm trying to tell you something here so that when you have children, you'll have a better understanding of things." While she was still listening to Miley's thoughts, terrified about them, she felt the moment that someone else sat down beside her. She told Molly. "That would be Tracy, a girl that has had it much rougher than Miley has, yet has gone through the same changes she is experiencing. They'll get this worked out. The two of them will. Not you."

"I was asked to go there by Mercy." Molly told her again that she would talk to Mercy. "If having kids is this much work, I'm not sure I want any."

"You'll have them, but you'll get to see them grow and develop into where those two are now. A daughter of yours will be with you forever, through changes that you can talk to her about. Never go to another parent's child to help them out, Piper. That is walking on dangerous grounds. What if you had said something about her mom? Something that you wanted to impart to her that would get Mercy in deeper trouble than she is now? Because you can't fix hormones."

"I'm not going to have any girls then. Fuck that shit." She dodged the smack to her head this time but didn't count on her smacking her hands. "You're very violent. Did you know that?"

"I do know that. I believe you bring that out in me." Molly smiled at her. "However, you should know that it's worse with boys. My goodness. They have their voices change, hair sprouting out in places they didn't before. They're half man and half child. They're ten times worse at puberty than girls are. But you know what? They get through it, and if you're anything like the mother I know you'll be, you'll have a better man than you might have thought."

Piper thought of the things she'd said to her niece. They weren't horrible, but they weren't very helpful either. Standing up, she sat back down because it occurred to her that she didn't have any idea how to fix this with her. Or even if there was a way to fix it. She looked at Molly. Piper truly did love this woman as she might well have loved a mom.

"I need your help." Molly said they all did. "Please help me. I know I should have...I will stay out of other families' troubles from now on. No matter how tempting it is to try and fix things."

"Go to Miley and tell her what you said to me. Tell her you messed up. Or whatever way you'd say that to her. I know you well enough to know that you can add color where it's not really needed." Piper kissed the older woman on the cheek. "Go on now. Take care that you hug her as well. She'll need that."

"I will." Piper started out the door and returned to hug Molly once again. When she pulled away, Piper told her something she knew the woman would get a kick out of. "Mercy had triplets. Two daughters and a son."

Then she left. Piper laughed as she shifted back to her bird then headed to Miley. It was just too much—the look on Molly's face was one that Piper would remember for the rest of her days.

Miley and Tracy were still at the dock. As soon as she landed and became her other self, Miley came to her and gave her a very strong hug. Piper hugged her just as tightly. Tracy joined them, but she was more gentle with hers. Piper knew the girl was still getting used to having people touch her. Tracy was shy for all her mouthiness.

"I'm stupid." Piper told Miley what she'd done in going to talk to Molly. "She told me Tracy was coming and that she was going to knock you around. I hope she didn't hurt you. This is all my fault."

"No, it's not. I mean, it is, but not really. You're going through some shit that I don't understand. I've never been a teenaged girl." They all laughed. "I'm sorry. I truly didn't mean anything I said to you. You hurt Mercy, and

I wanted to make you hurt too. I should have stayed out of it and left it to the two of you."

They made their way back to Mercy. She still hadn't told the girls about what had happened with Mercy, nor that Miley now had two sisters and a brother. She wanted to see the look on her face when she realized she had more than enough family for the three of them to care for. Sitting on the bed while they sorted out the gifts that were coming in, Piper watched Grant as he kept an eye on Joel. He was a little freaked out.

"I'm glad we have money." Grant asked Joel why that was going to be a problem. "The girls, they look like their mom, don't you think? Beautiful already. We're going to have to hire a full time crew to make sure that no boys come around them. That would include Miley. I've decided that none of them are leaving the house until I'm ready for them to date. Which will be never, I'm thinking. I'm not having anyone around my little girls until they're in their forties. Or older. That's why."

"What about your son? He's a handsome little guy." Joel growled at Grant when he spoke. "You do know that once he starts to notice girls, not a soul in the world will be able to keep him from them. You remember, don't you, Joel, what it was like to be a young man learning the ways of women?"

"That's precisely why none of them are going to go out with boys. Or men. Never." He looked at Miley, who was telling her sisters that Daddy was a poop head and that she'd show them the ropes. "You are forbidden to speak to your sisters and brother. That's it. I'm putting my foot down."

"Well, you'd better be picking it back up because I'm going to be with them as much as I possibly can." Miley stood up to her dad, toe to toe, and it was then that Piper realized how tall she'd gotten. "Don't try and do it, Dad. If you do, from what I've heard, you'll only make me want to disobey you even more. Now, we're not going to fight today. This is a great day for a celebration. Right, Dad?"

Joel looked at her and frowned. The poor man had three daughters he thought he could protect from everyone. Didn't the man realize he was married to the worst role model there ever was? Laughing when she stood up, she took the baby from Grant and sat on the bed again.

"Whatever the other aunts and your mom don't teach you, you can depend on Aunt Piper to teach you." She looked at Grant as she continued. "Now that your mom has shown us it's not that big of a deal to have a baby, then perhaps I can have you a cousin or two—"

"Holy shit. I just figured it out." Everyone turned to Duncan, who had been quietly standing back while the rest of them traded off babies. "Sorry. I was just thinking about the fact that you're all birds."

"Well, good for you. We've been birds for a long time now, dummy." Piper laughed when Mercy spoke. "Now that you've established what everyone else in this room already knew, what the fuck are you talking about? Or have you had a stroke? That would be a better reason than you just being tuned into the fact we've been—"

"How many eggs do you suppose a falcon would have, Mercy? In the event you're going to give me a smart assed answer, which you always do, they have three to four. You had three this time." He looked at her. "Piper? How many do you suppose a phoenix has? Again, three to four. You six, you're having children, but you're going to, I think, have them in batches."

"Batches? Did you just call my children a batch? You moronic fuck. I'm going to—"

Duncan backed away from the bed, holding the baby he had up as a shield.

"Hush, Mercy. I need to think." They all turned to Blaze, who had only just returned from her honeymoon with Bryson. "Hawks can have four to five eggs, I believe. Are you suggesting that I could have as many as five at a time?"

"I'm not sure. There aren't any books or information out there on birds, or for that matter, any kind of creature such as you guys are. For all I know, it could just be a coincidence. I guess we'll have to wait and see how many the next of you have. Is anyone here going to have a batch of babies?" Blaze raised her hand, as did Jude. Piper didn't know, didn't have the slightest idea how to tell if she was having a baby too. She looked at Grant, who shrugged. "Well, I guess in less than a year, we'll know for sure. I, for one, am happy about this. But then, it's not my body that is going through birth."

"Way to bring down a room, Duncan." He told them all he was sorry. As he made his way to Jude, Joel spoke again. "The thing we need to figure out is who we go to, to figure out this thing. As Duncan said, we are working with a lot of unknowns here. I think we were all wondering if there would be eggs born or not. That has been cleared up."

"Not necessarily." They then looked at her. "I mean, we are none of us the same sort of bird, right? For all we know, one or the rest of us could have eggs. Holy shit, this is scarier now than it was before. Too many unanswered questions if you ask me."

"Does this mean you don't want to have children?" She looked at Grant and smiled. "Good. I'm glad to hear that. However, there is nothing to worry about. Eggs or live births, one or five babies at once, we have the means and the magic to make it work out for all of us."

There was that. Piper went to Grant to have him hold her. She looked down at the bundle in her arms and wondered if she really cared how many she had. Or, for that matter, what their sex would be. She wanted to be a mom now. But it scared the shit out of her that she'd be terrible at it.

~*~

Grant was working on some paperwork when he

realized the house was quiet. Not that it wasn't like that most of the time, but he knew that Piper had been in the kitchen when he'd come in here, and she was then going to work. He reached out within the house and found nothing out of the ordinary. Reaching out beyond his home and to the castle grounds, he felt the presence of someone he didn't know. Getting up, he made his way into the front of the castle. The person standing there was very close to where the first squatter had been living. The ground was still bearing the marks of the trail of fire coming from Piper.

When Grant reached out to the man, he turned and looked at him. Grant hadn't any idea who the man was nor what he might be doing there. Walking slowly toward him, the man started in his direction as well. When they were still several feet apart, the stranger put out his hand.

"I'm Harold Bennington. Everyone calls me Harry. You and your wife own this land and the castle, I was told." Grant only stood there. "Yes, well, I don't blame you for being suspicious. I believe I would be, as well. I'm a professor at the college. Or I was until I retired recently. I wanted to find myself some sort of hobby that would take me around to places that few have been to before. When I was flying above this place a week or so ago, it just looked like barren land. It wasn't until I came by boat that I could see it's covered in magic. It's to keep out the unwanted."

"Yet here you are." Harry laughed as he nodded.

"You are here for what reason, Mr. Bennington? In the event you didn't understand the magic or the lack of a welcome mat being put out for you, you aren't welcome here."

"Yes, I understand. But there are circumstances I will explain to you. I was drawn here. I had a dream about this place, the people living here. It was a dream of a time I'd have no idea about. It was well before my time. When your Queen Dante lived here." Grant didn't say anything. "You have an excellent face, Lord Coby. It will keep me from playing cards with you. There were six birds in this dream. Six of the most wonderful creatures that had ever been. Larger than life too. The queen, your queen, made them her protectors. There are two more people that I dreamed about. The king, Duncan, and his wife, Judith. Everyone calls her Jude. Am I piquing your interest, Lord Coby?"

"You could have gotten any of that information anywhere, Mr. Bennington. I'm not saying that you've gotten it all right, but anyone around here— Well, perhaps not. We're a very protective lot here. What is it you want?" Bennington looked to his right, and he knew Piper was coming. "My wife. One of the birds."

"The phoenix. I know that because of her hair. My goodness, how do you keep from staring at such beauty all the time?" Grant didn't answer him, even if he had expected him to. "Hello, Lady Piper. It's wonderful to finally meet you."

Grant told her everything Bennington had told him. Piper put out her hand, and the man took it. Grant wasn't sure that was such a good idea. Not putting out his hand, he waited for Piper to tell him things were all right. Or not all right. She was stronger than he'd be any day of the week, and he knew it.

"Duncan is on his way. He said you were mentioned." If he understood what Piper said, the man only nodded. "I thought perhaps you were the mate to one of the two birds, but you're not, he assured me. Duncan said you are here for a reason that is in the books his mother left him."

"Yes. I dreamed about those as well. Not that I could read them, but I saw them in my dreams." Duncan landed on the ground beside him. He was still having difficulties in landing as the big bird, but he doubted anyone would notice but other birds. "My lord."

Bennington bowed before Duncan, and Grant noticed that Jude was coming as well. In the few minutes that Bennington was explaining to Duncan why he was there, the others landed close enough to be able to be part of the conversation. The man would either be dead in a very short time, or he'd be welcomed. It was entirely up to Duncan.

"My mother said you'd be joining us soon. Before fall was all she said. And that you were here to tell us about the antiques we're going to sell. She said you were a man to trust." Bennington thanked him. "No need for that.

Mom said you'd need us to put you up and to make sure you had everything you needed. She also said you'd be living here on this land, but within the walls of the keep, so you'd be safe. Mom didn't mention, however, what you would be safe from."

"I don't know either. I have no family. I've never been married. An only child of parents that were only children. I wonder too what she could have meant." Bennington looked around. "I guess since she said within the keep, you don't mean the castle. I don't think that is a place I'd like. I do tend to get cold a great deal."

"The keep is open, as well. When she said within the keep, she meant the walls surrounding the castle. We all have them." Piper pointed to the walls around their castle that encompassed acres of land where the castle stood in the center. "I believe your being here now is why several homes popped up when I came out to meet you. Dante knew a great many things, it appears."

They walked back to the castle, and there were indeed several homes now occupying the grounds. Grant wondered if the man would have to pick one of them, or the house would pick him. This was, he thought, one of the strangest things he'd encountered since he was a kid.

As soon as they were walking toward the homes, one of them appeared to have a door open. The closer they got to it, the home showed more welcoming things, such as a rocker on the front porch, a wreath on the door with Bennington on it, as well as someone just coming out of the door.

"My cook from my home on campus. Hello, Delia. I'd like to introduce you to the rest of the family we're now a part of." Harry laughed as he shook hands with the woman. "I'm so glad you agreed to join me here. It would have been lonely, I think, without you fussing at me all the time."

"I just popped into the kitchen. Like a jack in the box." Delia shook hands with all of them, taking his last. "Fae. As am I, your lordship. The mister here, he's got a bit of fae in him—long story, that one, but he didn't die that day. There are days when I'm tempted to do the deed myself, but we get along well enough. Mr. Harry is a vampire. Not as old as the rest of you seem to be, but he's hundreds rather than a thousand years old. such as you are."

"Thank you, Delia. I never thought to tell them that." Harry smiled at him. "I'm looking forward to getting to know you, Grant. The dream, as I was referring to before, showed you to be a good man and a person I could talk to."

"This dream, it seems to have given you a great deal of detail about all of us. While none of us, except for Duncan, knew anything about you. I'm not doubting yours or Duncan's word, but a little prewarning might have been helpful." They nodded, and Duncan said he'd been preoccupied a great deal since becoming a married man. "As a newly married man myself, I guess I can understand that."

They made plans to meet for dinner at their home. Since Piper had asked Blaze to come over and help them finish up the rest of the furniture around the house, they were prepared for guests. A lot of guests, as it turned out too.

He'd not realized that Blaze could take several pieces of different woods and make whatever kind of furniture she wanted. The woods would be shown in the pieces. That was why their dining room table was so beautiful. The cherry from the branches she used had made the grain so well thought out that it was hard for him to pass the room without going in to rub his hands over the gleaming surface.

They had beds and chests of drawers too. Bryson had helped him pick out the perfect woods to build an oversized barn in the keep. There Grant was going to store the gardening equipment, as well as other things that were needed to keep the area clean. Also, they had an incredible looking pen for the sheep when it got too cold for them to be out in the weather.

Things were coming together much faster than he thought they would. The castle was perfect for the two of them. Grant loved their living room. It was cool throughout the castle. Very much unlike any other stone building he'd ever been in. And sharing it with Piper was as good as it got. Last night, they'd talked about having children.

"I want as many as you wish to have." They both laughed. He started again. "I mean, whenever you want to start or stop, that will be the perfect amount of children for me."

"I don't know that I'd be a good mom. I don't have any experience with children. Just the few that have joined our family. And they're great. I'd hate to have the only pain in the ass children." Grant had pointed out to her that he'd bet even her nieces and nephews were pains. "Not when I see them."

"You see, that's the point. They're great around you because you're the cool aunt. I'm the extraordinary uncle. We get to see them at their best." She asked him if he thought he was that much of a big deal. "Yes. I do. And I'm going to keep on believing that right up until one of my kids breaks my heart. I know they will too. I certainly did my mom's a few times. Kids are assholes."

They laughed most of the night after that. Piper was someone that he wouldn't have thought to be his mate. They were so well suited it boggled his mind sometimes. She and he, they were wonderful at working together as well.

He'd never put much stock in having a family, a mate. Grant had watched the others, members of New Town, as their families grew. Some of them even came back to live there after they finished up college, or whatever had them leaving. When Piper came into his life, Grant knew he'd been mostly shocked rather than standoffish, as

Mercy had pointed out to him.

"Grant, can you come in here a minute?" He saved his document again. The way it was going today, he wasn't going to get much done. Grant went to see where Piper was. She was in the living room, and he asked her what he could do. "Look out there and tell me that you see the same thing I am seeing."

He didn't see anything at first but went closer to the window. It took him several seconds to find what she meant. Grant stared at the creature for a good long time before he realized what he was looking at. She asked him what that was.

"Fae. I don't know who it is, but I guess we can find out." Piper asked him if he was sure. "Yes. I've never seen one in their natural state. Usually, they're a lot like Mom and I are, human looking. Do you want to come with me to see what they want?"

"Yes. But just so you know, if there is any shit going down, I'm going to blast them to hell and back. I've had enough shit going on this week. I don't want to fuck up the rest of my day."

He laughed as he opened the door. Walking toward the tall fae, he waited until it turned towards him before he said anything. The need to submit was profound, and Grant felt himself fall to the ground and spread out so that the strong creature didn't harm him. He watched as Piper did the same. Holy Christ, he thought, what the hell was going to happen to them now?

# Chapter 9

Basil looked over the two he'd come to see. They were more beautiful than he'd been led to believe when he'd been told they were mated. Telling them to stand had the woman popping right up off the ground, but her mate, a fae such as he'd not seen in a long time, just stayed there.

"What are you doing?" He started to assure the woman he'd done nothing but come to see them, but she cut him off. "I don't know who you are, big guy, but as of right now, you're on my shit list. Who said you could come here and make us submit to you? I'm betting you thought this was a good idea all on your own. You mother fucking—"

"Piper, this is the king of the fae, Lord Basil. Your majesty, this is my wife and mate, Piper Coby. She's a phoenix that the queen of these lands changed many years ago." Basil put out his hand, and the woman slapped it away. "She's usually a great deal more friendly."

"Usually, I just kill sons of bitches that do what you did to me." Basil watched her face. She wasn't just angry but worried as well. With good reason, he thought. The king of her mate's kind hadn't made an appearance in more years than she'd been born. "What the fuck do you want?"

"Your help? I would ask for a drink too, but I believe you'd spit upon it. You are much more headstrong than I was told. I think I shall love talking with you." She crossed her arms over her breast and stared at him. "You'll not believe I heard the ground here had a great warrior. That you were also a woman that could be trusted with all manner of things. That is why I'm here. To ask a favor of you and your mate. You would be good for what I have to ask you."

"We're not getting any younger by you talking in riddles. Don't you guys send out minions when you're going to visit a place? You know, have the people you're going to ask something of be ready for you? I'd not think that simply showing up someplace has gotten you too much in the way of good neighbors, has it?" Basil laughed, and that seemed to piss her off more. She was a delight, and he was glad he'd done just what he'd done to see her. "I don't think you're the least bit funny. For the last time, what do you want?"

"For you to save my child." That shut her up. Basil wasn't sure, however, that it made her any more friendly.

"Would you allow me to sit down? Please?"

"Sure." Before she could put any kind of stipulations on his sitting, he took them both to his own home. Basil made sure he was well away from her before she realized what he'd done. "You mother fucker. You're just all kinds of stupid today, aren't you?"

Whatever he expected her to do, it wasn't for her to shift into a great bird and blow heat over him. It wouldn't harm him, but he knew that had he not already been prepared for her fire, he would have surely been hurt. Sitting in the chair that had been put there by him, he asked her to have a seat.

"You're not burning to a crisp." Basil laughed and told her he'd feel much better if she didn't seem so thoroughly disappointed. "But I am. You should be dead right now. That is a disappointment to me."

"I should hope that once you hear what I have to say, you'll change your mind. Please, my lady, have a seat. I wish to tell you what troubles I have and ask for you to help me with them. I do believe it is only the two of you that can save the faes of your world." Piper sat down, but she wasn't happy about it. She also told him she wasn't fae. "No. You're not fully a fae, but your mate is. I've been keeping an eye on Grant here since he took his first breath. I knew the queen of these lands quite well, too, as a matter of fact."

"Dante would have told us she was going to just pop in, as you haven't done." Basil laughed. He was sure she was upset with him, but he just couldn't help it. "Tell us what you have in mind. And don't think we didn't notice that you've taken us off our land. I don't know where I am, but I'm betting it'll burn just as quickly as anything on my side of magic."

"Yes. You're right. I will get right to the point then. My mate, Lady Rose, passed on. This was a great many years ago, I assure you. But at the time, I could only think what her not being here did to me." Piper told him she was sorry for his loss. "Thank you. It was a great many years ago. However, it doesn't mean I don't miss her at times. She was much like you, Lady Piper. Headstrong, and a woman that demanded courtesy. She also would have had my head had she had any idea what I did to you today. For that, I'm profoundly sorry. But as I said, I need your help."

"Whatever it is, I'm sure we can help you." Basil looked at Grant and nodded. "You said this had to do with your child. Have you only one?"

"I have none, as a matter of fact. That is where the two of you come in." Piper stood up, and Basil quickly went on to explain. "I don't wish for you to have my child, Lady Piper. No, not that. But to be a somewhat surrogate for it. It will be much easier than having to go to a physician to have you implanted with one, should that be the route we take. But I need only to touch the two of you, and you will go about creating the child on your own."

"I don't understand." He looked at Piper and asked her what she needed him to explain. "You just have to touch us, and then we're going to somehow carry you a child? That seems fishy to me. What's the catch?"

"Catch? Why none, I assure you. You will both be well paid for this. Very well." Piper said they didn't need money. "No. I suppose you don't. Then what is it you would require for you to help me? You see, I'm not long for my world. I only have a few thousand years left in which to train a child to do what is needed to care for the fae. I have, I'll honestly admit, been doing too much in order to keep things going. I should have approached someone before now. But had I done that, the magic would have likely killed the person that does such a job for me. The two of you are so strong it will not be an issue for either of you to carry the magic that would be required for you to carry a fae king."

Neither one of them said anything, at least to him. He knew they were talking to each other, however. When Grant looked at him sharply, he had a feeling his mate had figured out what was going on and told him. Basil, instead of telling him anything, called for refreshments to be brought to them. Then he confessed.

"I have less time than I told you, as I'm sure your mate has said. I will not see the birth of this child, nor will I be able to teach him the things he'll need to know to be a good ruler." Piper told him to tell them all of it. "Of course. Once I touch you, the two of you will not just have my child for me, the king that will someday replace me, but you'll be the king and queen of the faes until such time that your child will be able to take over. It is imperative that someone watches over the people here. Just as it was important for me to keep the lands safe for you and your family to come to take it. Dante, she knew I was dying even then."

"What caused you, the king of faes, to be so ill like this?" He wanted to sob to Piper, to thank her for her gentle tone. But he was a leader after all and needed to show them that. "You know, I could care less how strong you want us to see you. For all I care, you could be doing this on your deathbed. You might well be if you don't get to the fucking point."

Basil couldn't hold back; he did burst into tears. She was gentle and kind when it was necessary and hard when that was a better way to approach things. Just as his own mate. He got up to hand them the picture of his wife that had been painted so long ago. It made it easier for him; he thought if they could see what a wonderful person he'd lost.

"There was fighting among our kind for many years. Then when we weren't trying to kill each other, the humans would be fighting with us. It turned out that one of my own kind was the one that ended my reign. I was fed iron. So was my lady wife. She was with child when she was poisoned, to the point of her losing the babe. Then her own life was taken before it was figured out what had been going on. My own brother — he wished to be king in my place." Piper asked him if this bother was still alive. "Nay. My Rose killed him while taking her last breath. He is no more. But what he did beforehand, it's taken everything that we have held dear from us."

Piper got up and began pacing the room. He could feel the touch of her magic. Basil wasn't sure he could have stopped her, so he didn't try. She might well hurt him, and he just couldn't let that happen. Things depended on him telling them what was going on. When she stopped suddenly, he watched her.

"May I touch you?" He put out his hand, and she said she needed to touch his heart. "It's there where the iron is. I wish to see how much there is."

"Plenty, I'm told, to have killed a lesser fae." Basil stood up and opened his shirt for her. "I'm to understand that iron does not affect you. I wish I had thought of making that a reality for my family as well. Things would have been so — "

"Hush. I need to hear." He did so and watched her face. She had a lovely face, but expressionless too. She would defeat all with that look. No one would be able to tell if she was bluffing or that she had —

The pain took him to the floor. Crying out with it, he had to stay conscious enough to tell his guard to stand down. There wasn't even enough of his strength left to do that, as it turned out. Basil lay on the floor, his body aching so badly with each breath he took that he knew he was surely going to die. Begging for Grant to come to him so he might pass the magic on to him, the younger man stood over him and his mate to protect them. His guard stood down when Piper told them to get out of the room.

Basil woke. He didn't move for fear it would drain more of his strength away. There was so much to do right now, and he knew time was wasting. When a movement caught his eye, he turned toward it to see who was in the room. The candle being lit was all it took for him to see Piper sitting in the room with him.

"You're a fool. I'm sure that if you have good advisors, they have been telling you the same thing." Basil told her he thought they might be a little more afraid of him than she appeared to be. "I'm not afraid of you. Not at all. However, there are a few things you should know and a couple more that you need to worry about. Your brother isn't dead. He will be as soon as I find him, but for now, he'd still alive and kicking."

"No, I saw him die." Piper just cocked her pretty brow at him. "All right. For the sake of argument, he's still alive. Where has he been these past years? I'm sure you have an idea."

"I do. But I have other things to tell you first. You're not dying. At least not if you don't piss me off anymore. I've removed all the iron from your blood. Had you asked earlier, I could have done it a while ago." He asked her if she was sure. "Are you going to question my every statement to you? Or is it all right if we have question and answer time in a little bit? Your brother wasn't the only one that was poisoning you. It was someone in your household. Also, this is part of the things you need to know — your wife isn't dead, nor is the child. It's not your child, but your brother's."

He nearly told her she lied, but he had a feeling she'd hurt him. Basil sat up on the side of the bed and tried to work through what she was telling him. Thousands of questions went through his mind at one time.

"My wife, she was killing me as well." Piper said that was right. "And the child, you said he was my brother's. So when I would have died, my wife and her son would have come forth and taken over the kingdom."

"Yes. Any more tidbits you've worked out?" He could have easily hated her, but he didn't. Basil might well have fallen in love with her in the last few minutes. "You've already gone over it. Just say it, and I'll tell you if you're nearly as smart as everyone thinks you are."

"They're taking the money that is missing from the vault. The two of them have been robbing me while I thought them dead." She told him she'd already changed the locks on the vaults with her own magic. "Thank you. You said I'm not to die. What did you do?"

"As I said, I pulled the iron from your body, so it was no longer a threat." He could feel himself getting stronger by the minute. "The last thing you should know is that both Grant and I gave you some of our blood. I haven't any idea what it will do to you. Perhaps we can hope it made you smarter. But somehow I doubt that's going to be possible."

"Where is Grant?" She told him. "They think I'm dead? Why would you do that? There are people out there that are only loyal to me."

"Those people that you thought were loyal are now all dead. Yes, I killed them. Also, you will need another cook, as well as an advisor. You might say I have cleaned house for you." He didn't know what to say to her. Or even to ask of her. "The worrying part now. You will need to worry about your wife and brother. The child is all grown up, so he will also be a threat to you. While I can't find them, you can bet your ass that I will. Then they're going to meet an end that isn't nearly as nice as the rest of your staff had."

"I don't know what to say." He looked at her and saw that she was changing...evolving as well. "I touched you. You're fae."

"Yes. I was fucking pissed about that too, but I figure it's all magic. I have wings as well. So does Grant. Not happy about that. If I can't change into my phoenix, you're going to wish you'd never met me." He told her he wasn't so sure now. "Good. You keep that thought in your head all the time, and try not to piss me off."

"Thank you, Piper." She leaned forward, and he knew that whatever she was going to tell him, he didn't want to hear. "Is there more I should know?"

"Plenty. But for now, I'll tell you that all the money I could find that they've taken from the vaults is back. They're going to figure it out soon enough. Until I tell you differently, you're to stay in this room and only this one. It's been fixed, so no one will see or hear you so long as you're here. It's the only way to keep you from being hurt. You're weak now, as I'm sure you figured out. Until you're back to full strength, stay hidden. If you don't, I can no longer protect you."

"Why are you doing this?" Piper asked him what he meant. "You didn't have to do this. You could have just taken the job and let me die. Why? And why are you so angry about it?"

"I'm not angry at you, not really, but that you were letting yourself be made a fool of. That is not what a leader does. Yes, I had to do this. I don't know why, but I have this feeling that I was meant to help you and that it will, in some way, help the rest of us. As I said, I don't know why, but we'll see. If it's nothing, then that's all right too. You're alive to rule your lands, and I will have a favor from you."

"Anything." She told him to just get better for now as she stood up. "Piper, I literally owe you my life. Thank you."

He wasn't sure, but he thought she told him to fuck off as she left him there. Basil laid back on the bed and closed his eyes. It was funny, really. She was the most ungracious helper he'd ever met. Yet he had a feeling she'd kill for him. In fact, she'd already done that.

Basil let himself fall into a good deep sleep. He was safe, as was the castle and people while they were here. There wasn't anything more wonderful than that, he thought.

Before You Go...

# HELP AN AUTHOR

## *write a review*

# THANK YOU!

Share your voice and help guide other readers to these wonderful books. Even if it's only a line or two, your reviews help readers discover the author's books so they can continue creating stories that you'll love. Log in to your favorite retailer and leave a review. Thank you.

AWARD WINNING, BESTSELLING AUTHOR

Kathi Barton, a winner of the Pinnacle Book Achievement award as well as a best-selling author on Amazon and All Romance books, lives in Nashport, Ohio, with her husband, Paul. When not creating new worlds and romance, Kathi and her husband enjoy camping and going to auctions. She can also be seen at county fairs with her husband, who is an artist and potter.

Her muse, a cross between Jimmy Stewart and Hugh Jackman, brings her stories to life for her readers in a way that has them coming back time and again for more. Her favorite genre is paranormal romance, with a great deal of spice. You can visit Kathi on line and drop her an email if you'd like. She loves hearing from her fans. aaronskiss@gmail.com.

Follow Kathi on her blog: http://kathisbartonauthor.blogspot.com/